MALLORY VAYLE
AND THE
CURSE
OF
MAGGOTY
SKULL

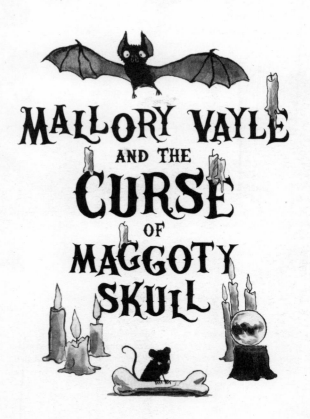

MALLORY VAYLE
AND THE
CURSE
OF
MAGGOTY SKULL

MARTIN HOWARD

Illustrated by
PETE WILLIAMSON

nosy crow

First published in the UK in 2024 by Nosy Crow Ltd
Wheat Wharf, 27a Shad Thames,
London, SE1 2XZ, UK

Nosy Crow Eireann Ltd
44 Orchard Grove, Kenmare,
Co Kerry, V93 FY22, Ireland

Nosy Crow and associated logos are trademarks and/or registered
trademarks of Nosy Crow Ltd.

ISBN: 978 1 80513 225 7

A CIP catalogue record for this book is available from
the British Library.

Printed and bound in Great Britain by Clays Ltd, Elcograf S.p.A.
following rigorous ethical sourcing standards.

FSC
www.fsc.org

MIX
Paper | Supporting
responsible forestry
FSC® C018072

1 3 5 7 9 10 8 6 4 2

www.nosycrow.com

For
Emma
M.H.

For
Pippa Howard
P.W.

CHAPTER 1

The brass handles and cherry-coloured wood of two coffins had been the only splashes of colour in the graveyard. As they sank into the earth, Mallory Vayle's world turned grey. Raindrops drummed on the umbrella above her head, the sound almost drowning out the young priest's voice.

"Ashes to … erm … ashes, is it?" he squeaked. "Yes, ashes. Dust to … ahh … what was it now? Mustard? No, dust. Dust. Of course. Sorry."

"Rubbish," snorted a woman's voice beside Mallory. "He's useless."

Mallory guessed it was the priest's first funeral. He kept forgetting the words. She didn't much care. To her, they

1

had less meaning than the wind blowing a dark lock of hair that had escaped her tight bun. She tucked it behind an ear. Ignoring the stuttering priest, she said a last – silent – goodbye to the bodies of her mother and father. It could have been worse, she told herself. Watching her parents being buried wasn't exactly putting the 'fun' in 'funeral', but it could have been worse.

"Are you all right, Mallory?" said the woman's voice at her side.

Mallory gave a small nod without looking round.

"Soon be over," said a deeper voice on her other side.

"I'm fine," she hissed between clenched teeth.

"That's my brave girl."

Yes, Mallory told herself. It could have been much, much worse. At least she had her parents to help her through this difficult time. Even if the ghosts of Sally and Lionel Vayle did insist on chattering through their own funeral as if they were at an afternoon tea party.

"Nice to see so many people turned up," said the wispy, see-through spectre of her father. He grinned around at the sea of black coats and umbrellas. "I mean, that's a worry, isn't it? What if no one comes to your funeral?"

"In this weather too," nodded Mallory's almost

transparent mother. "Poor things look drenched. That's one good thing about being dead, isn't it? The rain just goes straight through."

"I wish I'd died wearing slippers, though." Lionel Vayle looked down at the ghostly shoes he'd been wearing when the carriage he and his wife had been travelling in had taken an unexpected detour off Gibbett Bridge and into the river below. "These still pinch," he continued. "Which is odd, if you think about it. I mean, what exactly are they pinching if my toes are in that box down there? And why do I even have them on? Why are we dressed at all? Did our clothes die too?"

"I think we can all be very happy you still have clothes on, Lionel," his wife replied. "Oh, look, there's Sheila and Teddy Willetts at the back over there. We haven't seen them in ages."

"I mean to say, do I have to wear this suit for the rest of my ... umm ... I suppose I can't say 'life', can I?" mumbled her husband, digging a ghostly finger into his collar and tugging to loosen it.

His wife was too busy hopping up and down to answer. "Yoo hoo. Yoo hoo. Sheila," she shouted, waving.

"She can't see you," Mallory whispered. "No one can see you except me."

"Oh, yes," sighed Sally Vayle, dropping her hand. "Being dead is going to take some getting used to, I suppose."

Mallory sighed too, lifting her eyes from the twin, coffin-shaped holes. The graveyard was packed with crooked gravestones, covered with ivy and scattered between trees that were grimly hanging on to their last leaves. The tombs had been hemmed in by a wall of stone. Over it, the windows of steep-roofed houses stared into the graveyard.

The priest stuttered on, robes lashing in the wind.

"He really is terrible," said her mother.

"The whole experience is disappointing," Lionel Vayle agreed. "What you want at a funeral is drama. Wailing and gnashing of teeth. People sobbing into hankies and tearing at their clothes. Weeping mourners throwing themselves on to the coffins. I'd give the whole thing three out of ten."

"Da, are you giving your own funeral a review?" Mallory whispered.

Her father's train of thought wasn't going to be derailed. "What you want," he continued, "is people crumpling to their knees under the weight of their grief and mysterious strangers turning up ... like that one. Oh. Who's she?"

Mallory's gaze followed her father's ghostly pointing finger to see a stranger walking through rows of

5

gravestones. She stopped a little way apart from the crowd. A few people turned to look. The woman was odd: tall, and strangely dressed beneath a bent umbrella. She wore a black turban with a stuffed crow attached to the front. Most of her face was hidden behind a large pair of spectacles like none Mallory had ever seen before. The glass lenses were black. The rest of the stranger was also hidden beneath a black fur coat. "I've no idea," Mallory said, answering her father's

question from the corner of her mouth.

"Ooh, this is more like it," he chirped. "A mysterious stranger turning up just when you need one, eh? Dark, forgotten secrets coming back to haunt us even as our bodies are lowered into the earth. *Classic* funeral."

The ghost of Sally Vayle peered at the woman. Her jaw fell open. "No," she gasped. "No ... it can't be..."

Mallory's father interrupted. "They've started shovelling earth over us, Sally. Should we pay our last respects to ourselves?"

"Seems a bit pointless, Da," Mallory whispered. Even so, she fell silent, bowing her head while mud splattered on to the lids of her parents' coffins and her world turned cold and grim. Her ghostly parents could no longer do important parenting things, like earning money and putting food on the table. The Browns down the street had taken care of her after the accident, but they had six children of their own and no space for another. She was headed into the city orphanage and the loveless care of its grim matron.

Tears welled in her eyes.

Stop it, she scolded herself. Her parents were dead. Nothing she could do would change that. But at least she

still had her parents. She would always have her parents now. They would never change, never grow old.

And never, ever again would she feel their arms around her.

As the priest stammered through his last words, umbrellas started drifting away from the crowd. Funeral over, Mallory looked up to see people walking towards her. First to grip her hand was a plump man with greasy hair beneath a bowler hat.

"I'm so sorry for your loss … erm … Molly, isn't it?" he said. "If there's anything we at the bank can do…"

"Eh?" said Mallory, snapping out of her thoughts.

"Mr Whuppley, my old boss," her dad whispered in her ear. "Tell him he's an ugly, short-tempered git, would you, Mall? The best thing – the very best thing – about being dead is not having to see his greasy face every day. Tell him everyone at the bank knows about his bum problem too. We've all seen him scratching."

"Bum problem?" said Mallory without thinking. "Scratching?"

Mr Whuppley's face turned white. "Wha … *what*? Who's got a bum problem? I don't have a bum problem," he gurgled.

"Sorry. I meant to say, that's kind of you, Mr Whuppley," Mallory said hurriedly while her dad had hysterics next to her.

"Shush, Lionel," said Mallory's ma absently. She was still staring at the woman in the turban. "Oh, cripes," she muttered. "I think it is her."

Taking no notice of her parents, Mallory shook hand after hand until the graveyard was empty.

Almost empty.

Mallory blinked. Not all the mourners had left. The woman in the turban and strange spectacles was walking towards her, a hand outstretched.

"Mallory," said her mother. "This is—"

"You must be Mallory, darling girl," interrupted the woman in a loud voice, clasping Mallory's hand, then dropping it. Tossing aside her umbrella, she dragged Mallory into the depths of her coat instead. "What am I *thinking*?" she cried. "Shaking hands won't do at all. I simply must have you in my arms this instant. It's an instinct, isn't it? Even the mother earwig clasps her young to her earwiggy bosom."

Her own umbrella knocked aside, Mallory screwed her face up as cold rain trickled down the back of her dress.

"Mmmf-mmmf," she squawked from deep within the fur.

"*Enough,*" bellowed the woman, pushing Mallory away and holding her at arm's length. Fingers like talons gripped her shoulders. "Let me look at you. Let me see that face. That face so ruined by grief; so horribly, horribly wrecked by sorrow."

Deciding to let that pass, Mallory wiped rain from her eyes. Steadying her umbrella in a sudden gust of wind, she said, "Umm ... who are you, exactly?"

"She is—" Sally Vayle began.

The strange woman interrupted again. "But you mustn't weep, my sweet, sweet girl." Releasing one of Mallory's shoulders, she pulled dark glasses halfway down her nose. Violet eyes peered over the rims into Mallory's, as she continued. "For what is death but the blowing out of a candle? A candle no longer needed because dawn has arrived?"

"Who's Dawn?"

"Exactly, my darling. Exactly. Whose dawn indeed? How right you are." The woman leaned closer. The stuffed crow on her turban pecked Mallory's forehead. "Tell me, child, do you have it?" she asked in a whisper.

"Do I have what?" Mallory asked, baffled. "A sudden

urge to run away, screaming?"

"Do you have the family gift?" the woman hissed, gripping tighter. "The family *curse*. The talent to part the curtains of death itself and speak with those who have passed over."

Mallory opened her mouth, but the woman was still jabbering. One hand reaching dramatically to her forehead, she cried, "No, wait. Don't tell me. Even now my spirit guide, Mr Lozenge, whispers to me from the beyond. He tells me—"

It was Mallory's turn to interrupt. One word stood out from the woman's babble, and was honking at the front of her brain. "Family?" she said, blinking.

"As I was saying," said the ghost of Sally Vayle, sounding annoyed. "She is—"

"Family," repeated the woman. "Dear girl, I am your Aunt Lilith."

"—your Aunt Hilda," finished Mallory's mother. "My sister. My long *lost* sister."

CHAPTER 2

Mallory goggled at the woman. "Aunt Hilda?" she gasped. "Aunt? Aunt as in ... *aunt*?"

A pained look flickered over her aunt's face. "It's *Lilith*," she insisted. "We don't use the 'H' word. But, yes, my tear-stained poppet. I am your aunt. A guardian angel sent by destiny in this beastly time of tragic despair."

Mallory blinked, open-mouthed, as her aunt prattled on.

"I only discovered that poor Sally had died this very morning," she was now saying, flapping a hand. "It took some days for your parents' lawyer to discover I even existed. Imagine my astonishment when I found I had a niece, alone and quite desperate – *frantic* – for a companion to lead her through this awful time of heartbreak and loss. Darling, I flew here to be at your side, but not before making certain arrangements. Papers are being prepared as we speak."

"Excuse me," said Mallory. "Are you saying…"

Her aunt nodded. "Yes. Yes, you poor bedraggled soul. You are coming to live with me."

"Eeek," squealed Sally Vayle.

"I have an aunt," Mallory spluttered. She glanced at her parents' ghosts. "Why did no one tell me?"

"Yes," said her father. "Why did no one tell her? Why did no one tell *me* either?"

"I haven't seen Hilda since I was a fifteen," Sally Vayle protested. "I … err … well, I sort of forgot about her. She was always an embarrassment. Floating around the house, twittering on about spirits, going into trances at the breakfast table and whatnot. I did my best to ignore her but it was a relief when she left home."

"Sally and I were never as close as sisters should be, I'm afraid," said Aunt Lilith at the same time, also in answer to Mallory's question. "As a young girl your mother was quite overawed by my spiritual talents. It must have been terribly painful for her to see my powers blossom while

she remained so dreary and ordinary. I used to call her 'Lumpy', you know."

Sally Vayle squawked. "She did too. I'd forgotten that. The cheek! The absolute nerve."

"My ma's not lumpy," said Mallory.

"Thank you, Mallory."

"It was just girlish silliness," Aunt Lilith went on, with another wave of her hand. "Our roads parted years ago. Just as I predicted, Lumpy's life remained dull and uninteresting while my own path led me ever deeper into the strange wonders of the spirit realm."

"You're a psychic?" asked Mallory, blinking up at her aunt.

"Yes, my dear. The universe has gifted me with that shadowy talent. I walk the half-world, bending my ear to the whispers of those who have passed over."

Sally Vayle snorted, waving a ghostly hand in front of her sister's face. "Hello," she shouted. "Hello, Hilda! Can you hear me? Hmph. No, didn't think so. Don't believe a word of it, Mallory. She's as psychic as your father's underwear."

"Do we have to bring my underwear into this?" Lionel Vayle chipped in. "We're at a funeral, it's hardly

appropriate." He paused, then added, "Though I did sometimes wonder if it had a touch of voodoo."

"Yes, dear, a dark stain of evil," his wife batted back. To her daughter, she said, "Hilda's right about one thing, though. She is your only living family. If she's having the paperwork drawn up, I'm afraid we're stuck with her."

Mallory nodded. Aunt Hilda, or Lilith, or whatever she called herself, was obviously bonkers. Even so, she was family and family beat the orphanage. With a sideways glance at her ma, she murmured, "She'll have to do."

"Did you say something, darling?" asked her aunt.

"Yes," Mallory replied. "I said it's nice to meet you, Aunt Hil— *Lilith*, but I'm cold and wet and it's been a horrid day. May we go home?"

"Oh, my poor, sweet girl," yelped Aunt Lilith. "What must you think of me? Here I am feasting on the sight of you while you're shivering like a wet lettuce. Come, let us flee this dismal place." Pushing dark glasses back up her nose, she retrieved her shabby umbrella and shook it out. Gripping Mallory's shoulder, she spun her and gave her a gentle push towards the cemetery gates where a carriage stood waiting, the horses tossing their heads and snorting impatiently.

"You didn't answer my question, by the way," Mallory's new aunt said as their feet crunched on the gravel path. "*Do* you have the family gift? *Can* you talk to the dead?"

Mallory flicked her eyes towards the ghosts of her parents floating along beside her. Biting her lip, she shook her head, mumbling, "No." Changing the subject, she added, "Where is home, anyway?"

Her aunt chuckled. "Home, my dear, is Carrion Castle. It's a darling place. Simply darling."

CHAPTER 3

Horses snorting, hooves clattering, the hired coach rattled down cobbled streets. Bucking in her seat, Aunt Lilith babbled over the noise, twittering about spirits and her own tremendous psychic powers. Murmuring interested noises in what she hoped were the right places, Mallory shifted her backside and adjusted her funeral dress, then she turned her head to look out of the window, watching the city go by and listening to the clatter of iron-bound wheels. The rain had stopped but evening was closing in. Lights were appearing in windows. Gasmen climbed ladders to ignite street lamps.

Aunt Lilith leaned forward to touch Mallory's knee. "Would you like a demonstration, dear? I could ask

Mr Lozenge, my spirit guide, to summon the spirits of your mother and father."

"What?" Mallory turned to stare at her aunt.

"I could reach out to the spirit realm and pass messages from your parents," her aunt repeated. "Really, it's no trouble and it might help you be at peace with their horrific deaths."

In the seat next to Mallory, her mother rolled her eyes. "I can't wait to hear this," she said. "Go on, then, Hilda. My first message is that you're a fraud. Did you hear that? I said, YOU'RE A DISGRACEFUL FRAUD."

Unaware that her sister was bellowing in her face, Aunt Lilith leaned back in her seat, her eyes rolling upward. "Oooh, Mr Lozenge," she droned, raising her hands to the cab's ceiling. "Dear guide, we seek two spirits who have recently passed: Sally ... and..." She stopped and glanced at Mallory. "Sorry, dear. What was your father's name?"

Through clenched teeth, Mallory said, "Don't. I mean, thank you but I'd rather you didn't."

"Oh, come on, Mallory. I could do with a laugh..." Lionel Vayle stopped, and then pointed out of the window, chirping, "Ooh, look, Sally. Isn't that where we died?"

"Lionel!" squealed his wife. "What are you thinking? Don't look, Mallory."

Too late. Mallory was already looking. While her aunt had been speaking, the coach had rolled on to Gibbett Bridge where it had become caught in traffic. A few feet away, Mallory could see a broken gap in the stone barrier where – for reasons known only to themselves – the horses pulling her parents' carriage had leapt into the river. The coach itself, the passengers and a very surprised driver, had crashed through behind them, plunging into the icy depths below. After the accident, a police inspector had visited Mallory at the Browns' house to report that witnesses had seen nothing suspicious. The police, he had said, were working on a theory they called, 'Very Stupid Horses'.

"Really, Lionel. If you weren't already dead I'd strangle you," said Sally Vayle. "Mallory, sweetheart. Look at me. There's nothing to see."

Mallory ignored her. Staring at the broken stone that marked her parents' fatal crash, a tear trickled down her cheek. A small frown creased her forehead. She shivered. On the very edge of her senses she felt a distant, fading, wrongness. Maggots wriggled in the pit of her stomach.

While her aunt babbled, Mallory whispered quietly to her mother, "What happened there?"

Sally Vayle's ghost shrugged. "It was all very fast, dear. No point dwelling on it, eh?"

With a jerk, the hire cab started forward again. Aunt Lilith continued, leaning forward: "Are you sure, dear? I'm definitely feeling Lumpy."

Mallory started in her seat as her aunt touched her knee. She dragged her attention away from the last place her parents had been alive. It took a few seconds to work out her aunt still talking about contacting her parents' spirits. "I'm sure, thank you," she said, blinking away another tear and catching hold of a hanging strap as the coach took a sharp right turn into narrower streets. This was a part of the city Mallory had never explored – a district known as Stabbings, for the simple reason that there were a lot of stabbings in its dark alleys. Heart thumping, she sat up again and peered out of the window. Buildings closed in on the rattling coach. Here, they were older – the overhanging upper storeys of houses forming a tunnel with only a crack of dark sky to be seen between them; the windows so close that people

on opposite sides of the street could reach out and steal a pillow from their neighbour's bed. No street lamps lined the roads here, just a few dim lanterns in the windows of shops full of junk and third- and fourth-hand clothes.

Mallory watched the Dead Cosy funeral parlour go past. The coach passed the cobwebbed windows of Grimm Books where the window display was the drunk owner sleeping on a pile of spineless books with a spilled bottle in his hand.

Deeper into Stabbings the streets became even darker.

"Here we are, then. Home sweet home," said her aunt eventually. While she paid the coach driver, her niece climbed down from the cab into a small alley. Mallory's boots clicked on cobbles, the sound muffled by fog, which sulked around her ankles like grumpy porridge. Above, clouds parted, revealing a full moon that turned the alley black and silver. Houses slumped, their roofs buckled and uneven and missing great patches of tiles, their windows smashed or boarded over. A sign hung crookedly on the wall. It read: Nightmare Alley.

Her mother and father floated down next to her. "Oh, my," said Sally Vayle, looking up.

"Jeepers," hissed Lionel Vayle, also craning his neck

21

to stare upwards.

Mallory turned to see what they were looking at. She gulped. Behind overgrown creepers a cliff-face of a house leaned over her, so old it looked like it had grown there; a relic from a forgotten time, hidden when the city grew up around it. The arched front entrance gawped like a hungry mouth. Hideous gargoyles sprouted from the battlements.

Battlements?

Mallory took a step back in surprise. Despite the name, she had not been expecting Carrion Castle to be an actual castle. After all, back on her old street the Fearnley Family had called their small cottage Fearnley Towers. The Chubbs had named theirs Chateau Chubb. But Carrion Castle was, in fact, a proper castle. A very *spooky* castle. Once again, maggots wriggled in her belly. Fingernails dragged down the chalkboard of her soul. Something about the place made her feel weak in the bladder area. If the castle had hands they would have been bony, gnarled hands and it would have been rubbing them together in sinister glee. The mansion oozed a spite that twisted Mallory's insides. Whatever was inside felt hungry. Old. Evil.

A colony of bats burst from a crumbling tower, circling it in the moonlight.

"I forbid you to go inside, Mallory," said her mother. "It's … it's… Something's not right."

"It's making my skin crawl and I haven't even *got* skin," added her father.

Mallory nodded in agreement. The place was a ghost story waiting to happen.

Which would have been fine. Mallory had been seeing – and ignoring – ghosts for as long as she could remember. It was a secret only she and her parents had known. There were usually one or two floating around, doing whatever it was ghosts did. Most of them were a bit gloomy. Mallory assumed this was because they didn't have a lot to look forward to except staring out of windows and going "woo" occasionally. Ghosts were of no real interest, just a wispy part of Mallory's landscape that had long ago lost any power to frighten her.

Until now.

She swallowed. "Umm… Aunt Hil… I mean, Lilith," she said as her aunt climbed down behind her. "Is this your home?"

"*Our* home, dear," said Aunt Lilith. "Carrion Castle.

I inherited it a few years ago in mysterious circumstances, you know."

"I'm not going in there," Mallory told her.

Her aunt stepped back, blinking. "But why ever not?" she asked. "It's a darling old place. Full of history and charm and—"

"Hatred," Mallory interrupted. "This house is haunted."

Mallory winced as her aunt clapped her hands together, squeaking with glee and jumping up and down on the spot. "But how simply *marvellous*, you precious, precious girl," she crowed. "You sense spirits, don't you? You *do* have the family gift. I knew it. You can't hide it, you know. Not from me. To think such an extraordinary child could come from Lumpy's dreary tummy."

Mallory hugged herself, gazing up at the castle. "Can you please not call my mother 'dreary'?" she said.

"Yes, yes, my lamb," her aunt replied with the flap of a hand. "Dear Aunt Lilith is just so excited. But why ever did you say you had no talent?"

Mallory bit her lip. "I ... err ... I'm cold," she said, changing the subject.

"Of course you are. *Brrr.* Come along, darling. Let's get out of this absolute weather before we catch our deaths."

Taking an enormous iron key from the pocket of her fur coat, Aunt Lilith walked up the steps to the arched front door.

The ancient, rusty mechanism clanked.

With the gloomy creak of a tomb, the front door opened.

Beyond, all was darkness.

Mallory wrapped her arms around herself, shivering. She had no choice. The coach was already rattling away and she had nowhere else to go. A strange aunt and this ruined castle were all she had. If she didn't go inside she would freeze on the murderous streets of Stabbings.

Taking a deep breath, she stepped into darkness.

Unseen, a patch of shadow looked down from the narrow window of the castle's highest tower.

CHAPTER 4

Goosebumps crawling down her spine, Mallory followed her aunt into the castle. With a gulp, she pulled the door closed behind her. Just inside, she stopped – heart thudding – while Aunt Lilith took off her dark glasses in the darkness. Mallory heard a *click* as she folded them into a pocket.

A match flared. Mallory shivered again as the spark cast terrifying shadow creases on Aunt Lilith's face. The crow on her turban glared at Mallory with a look of deep, deep disapproval.

Her aunt lit a candle. Golden light spread, painting the scene in shadows. The castle's hallway was vast: impossibly grand and dismally rundown at the same

time, like a ruined church. The floor was a chessboard of stained tiles. Paint peeled from the walls – lighter patches showing where paintings had once hung. A vast, unlit chandelier dripped cobwebs. Two sweeping staircases led to the upper floors.

Mallory heard her mother make a noise of disgust behind her. "Good grief. Hilda was always messy but would it have killed her to push a duster around?"

"Cobwebs," Mallory murmured, pushing dusty webs aside. Inside, the haunted feeling was worse. She and her aunt were not alone. She couldn't see any ghosts, but she could sense a presence: a cold, spiteful presence. Skin prickled on the back of her neck. Something was watching her. She was sure of it. Something was hideously gleeful to see her. She could almost – *almost* – hear cackling laughter.

"I'd never heard of the place until I found out it was mine," Aunt Lilith prattled. "The lawyer – Dirtfinger, I think his name was – didn't tell me much. Just that an anonymous benefactor had left it to me. It was all very strange, but you don't ask questions when someone hands you the keys to a castle, do you? The local people believe a wicked witch used to live here. Isn't that simply *delightful*? Like something out of a fairy tale."

Mallory didn't answer. A shadow flickered on the wall. Again, her stomach twisted. Just as it had on Gibbett Bridge. This time the sense of rotting evil was stronger. Much, much stronger.

Lighting another candle, Aunt Lilith passed it to her niece, giggling. "I find the cobwebs strike exactly the right tone. My customers expect a certain atmosphere, you see. The mood has to be just right for my psychic work and this old place *oozes* supernatural."

Mallory looked around. Just inside the door, by her head, hung a corkboard, pinned with curling pamphlets. Lifting her candle with a trembling hand, she peered at one.

NEWS OF THE WEIRD
This Week's Messages From Beyond the Grave

DEATH BY PIE

Robert Spoonlove, who lived at Pugney Lane until his death last year would like his family to know it was Mildred's fish pie that killed him, just like he always said it would.

KILL BILL

Nora Thompson misses her husband, Bill, and cannot wait until they are reunited once more in death. She wonders if someone would kindly push him down the stairs.

DEAD, ACTUALLY

Nanna Ginny would like everyone at Number Ten to know that she's not 'just having a nap'. She's been dead for three months now and is a bit upset that no one has noticed.

If you enjoyed these messages, don't forget to
book a sensational Psychic Reading with
LILITH NIGHTSHADE.
Ask inside for our special offers!

"Oh, I see you've found my little news sheet," Aunt Lilith twittered on. "I write it myself, you know. Every week. It brings such comfort to the poor souls left behind by departed loved ones."

Mallory opened her mouth to speak, but the words caught in her throat. On the edge of hearing, whispers fluttered the cobwebs, the words too faint to hear. In the depths of the castle, a door slammed. For an instant, she thought she caught a part of a word – *"...mancer"* – long and drawn out and filled with sinister triumph.

"We do have a small problem with draughts," said Aunt Lilith calmly.

"There's something here," Mallory whispered, her voice shaking.

"I did say the old place is crammed with spirits, didn't I?" giggled her aunt. "But nothing to worry about. Aunt Lilith is here to protect you and they're all quite friendly."

"No. No, they're not," Mallory answered firmly. "They're not friendly at all. Aunt Lilith, I would prefer to stay at the city orphanage, if you don't mind."

Lit by golden candlelight, a pained expression crossed her aunt's face. "Well, really, darling, you might at least make a small effort." Seeing her niece about to protest, she lifted a finger. "Auntie Lilith insists. Come along, you've had a ghastly, *ghastly* day and I'm sure everything seems a little on the gloomy side just now. But a good night's sleep will make everything better. Let me make a nice cup of herbal tea and show you to your room. No, no, don't say another word."

Mallory gritted her teeth. After the long journey from the graveyard it was getting late. She would have to spend at least one night in Carrion Castle. Anger welled up inside her. She hated that this was what her happy, cosy life had turned into: a haunted castle and a fraud of an aunt.

"We'll take care of you, Mall," her father's ghost whispered as if he could read Mallory's thoughts.

Her mother nodded. "Yes. Hilda's right about one thing: everything will seem better in the morning. Until then, we won't move from your side. Tomorrow we can start sorting this mess out."

Mallory looked up into her aunt's violet eyes. "One night," she whispered. "That's all."

CHAPTER 5

"Mallory."

Mallory awoke with a start at the sound of a voice calling her name. She sat up, looking around. The room her aunt had shown her to – Mallory refused to think of it as *her* room – was lit by a soft beam of moonlight struggling through a dirty window. She gasped. Her parents' ghosts were gone. She had fallen asleep with one of them sitting either side of the sagging, damp four-poster bed. Both had promised they would not leave.

Now they were gone.

"Ma," she called out gently. "Da?"

"Mallory."

Again, the voice slithered around the room. Unearthly. Rotten-sounding. Without stopping to wonder if this was something she should ignore – perhaps even going so far as to pull the covers over her head and whimpering a little – Mallory scrambled from the bed, struck a match, lit a candle and crossed the room. Wearing an enormous old nightdress her aunt had lent her until her own belongings had been collected, she looked like a candle herself; a candle that had half-melted into a mound of ruffled wax.

Behind her, a shadow that had no right to be there flitted across the wall.

Mallory opened the door, peering down an empty corridor. "Ma," she called out again. "Where are you?"

"*Coooome.*"

The word was a whisper, coming from the grand entrance hall below. It sounded distant and cracked and ancient, and definitely wasn't the voice of either her mother or her father.

"*Maaaaallory.*"

Mallory swore under her breath. Louder, she said, "Where are my parents?"

A long chuckle echoed around the house.

Mallory paced to the top of the stairs. Enough was enough. The minute she found her parents, she was leaving. Feeling anger bubbling up from her stomach to the roots of her hair, she repeated, "Where are they?"

"...where ... where ... where..."

Her words had a strange vibration to them, on the edge of an echo. "Tell me now or I'll... I'll..." She stopped. What could she do to a ghost?

"Maaaallory," crooned the voice. Behind her, a shadow moved.

On the other hand, she decided, what could a ghost do to *her*? Ghosts were literally nothing. Wisps of what had once been that refused to take the big hint death had given them. They had no power. She had spent her life walking past and sometimes even through them. Ghosts were just a minor annoyance.

"Fine," she hissed, holding the candle high. Its small flame streamed behind her. "If it will make you bring my ma and da back, I'm coming."

"Maaaaaaaaallllorreeeeeee."

Holding her candle high, Mallory stepped down the wide staircase into Carrion Castle's hall.

"Cooooome."

The voice seemed to be coming from a patch of wall which had been wallpapered over many years ago. Most of the paper was hanging off. Crossing checkered tiles, Mallory reached out and tore a strip, then jumped back with a start when the whole sheet slipped off damp plaster and landed with a pluff at her feet.

Mallory let out a scared *eep*. Directly in front of her, picked out in dark brown stains, was the unmistakable shape of a grinning skull.

It stared back at her, a grin on its fleshless face.

"What's wrong with this house?" she whispered.

"Mallory!"

The slithering voice sounded demanding now. Without being told, Mallory knew there was something behind the wall. Something the voice wanted her to find. She gritted her teeth. If the answer to her parents' disappearance lay beyond this wall then she had no choice but to go through it.

Mallory attacked the plaster, digging into it with bare fingernails. It had been slapped on thickly, and a long time ago. Small lumps began to fall around her ankles. Not fast enough. She picked up a nearby chair and smashed it on the tiles. It shattered. Snatching up a leg, she used the

pointy end to gouge at the plaster instead. More dropped away. Soon, a small pile had built up around her ankles. Still she hacked until – with a final, dusty thump – what was left crashed to the floor.

Breathing hard, she dropped the chair leg.

Behind the jagged hole in the plaster was a door.

She pushed it.

The door swung open with a tortured squeal.

Stench rolled up from the darkness below. Air that had been trapped for hundreds of years rushed at her. For a few seconds, Mallory could hardly breathe. It felt like she was being suffocated with an old man's trousers. She picked up her candle. It trembled in her hand. Squeezing her eyes shut for a moment, she forced herself to stop shaking. "Ghosts can't hurt me," she reminded herself as she took a step into the dark. Steadying herself with one hand on the damp stone wall, she walked down slippery steps, whispering, "Ma? Da? Are you down here?"

Darkness swallowed her. A rat scuttled across her path. With an *"eww"* of disgust, she jumped back and stumbled. Falling, she managed to catch her candle. It fluttered dangerously. "Don't go out. *Please* don't go out," she yelped.

The flame steadied.

Mallory found the bottom of the steps. "So far, so awful," she murmured to herself, peering along a dark passage. She squealed again, certain she'd caught a glimpse of shadow moving from the corner of her eye. Telling herself it was her imagination and trying to ignore the pounding of her own heart, she crept on, peering into rooms that had been left undisturbed for hundreds of years, finding only rotten furniture and mouldy paintings. There was no sign at all of her parents' ghosts.

Sloping passageways and twisting stone stairways led her further down into the labyrinth.

How am I going to find the way back?

The maze beneath Carrion Castle seemed endless, but eventually Mallory turned a corner, and found herself in a part of the labyrinth that had clearly once been a dungeon. The passage ahead was lined with cells barred with iron. At the end of the row stood a door fastened with rusty padlocks. Planks of wood had been nailed across it. Dripping paint spelled the words: STRANGER: TURN BACK. DO NOT OPEN THYS DOOR.

"You have got to be *joking*," Mallory hissed while fear twisted her intestines into a balloon poodle.

Beneath the painted words, a painted skull grinned at her.

Shadows shifted around her. *"Maaaalllory,"* the voice whispered in her ear, urging her to go on. To open the door.

"Ma? Da?" Mallory tried again.

The only answer was the distant skittering of rats, and a drip-drip-drip of water. Carefully setting down her candle, murmuring encouragement to herself, Mallory stepped forward and tugged at a padlock. Rusted through, the iron crumbled. Chains clattered to the floor. With more effort, she pulled away rotten planks, and lifted the heavy bar across the door.

With a puff of dust, it fell at her feet.

Taking a deep breath, Mallory leaned her shoulder against the wood and shoved.

The door opened more easily than she'd expected. Showered in dust, rust and chips of stone, she tumbled into the room beyond, falling to her hands and knees into the tiny chamber – a prison cell lined with stone blocks, green with mould and slime.

Scrambling to her feet, Mallory banged her head on the low ceiling. Hissing, "Ouch," she looked around.

41

The room was empty except for a chest that looked like it might contain pirate treasure.

"*Maaaaaaaaalllooorrry.*"

The voice sounded like it was pleading now. It wanted her to open the chest.

Knowing that if she stopped to think about what she was doing she would run screaming back into the maze, Mallory gripped the lid and heaved.

With a coffin-lid groan, it opened.

Ancient hinges fell apart at the sudden movement. The lid fell away in a crash of wood.

Mallory looked down.

She opened her mouth.

Nothing came out but a dry, rattling wheeze.

Nestled on rotten sacks in the bottom of the chest lay a human skull. A skull without a body, the white bone discoloured and patchy with age.

Black, lifeless eye sockets stared up at her.

Sockets that were suddenly not lifeless at all.

Mallory's ragged breathing stopped completely as two tiny points of green light flared, staring at her from the depths of the skull.

The lights brightened: intense as poison, as distant as

stars. Mallory could feel them burning into her own eyes. Unable to look away, she could only scream a soundless, rasping scream.

"Hullo, hullo, hullo," said the skull. One of the green lights in its eye sockets blinked off and on again in a wink. "Pip pippety pip. Lovely day for it. Ahoy there, m'hearty. Hoo-ray, and up she rises."

"Wh-*what*?" said Mallory, feeling like her brain was melting. "What are you talking about? Who are you?"

"Well, excuuuuuse me," chattered the skull. "Please allow me to introduce myself. *Woo woo*. Drum roll, please ... b'dum tish ... *aaaand* ... you can call me Maggoty. Maggoty Skull."

"Muh-muh-muh Maggoty Skuh-Skull?"

"No, just Maggoty Skull. Yup, yup, yup. That's me. Mad, bad and dangerous to know. Wicked? Well, yeeeees, but basically – you know – *fabulous*. You gotta sprinkle a bit of glitter on it, don't you? Give 'em a show. Give 'em a SHOOOOW."

Maggoty Skull paused. "Oh, you've fainted. *Sheesh*. Get a grip, guuurl. Hello. HELLO. Wakey, wakey. Up and at 'em. Things to do. Curses, wigs and all kinds of dark doings."

CHAPTER 6

Mallory opened her eyes and sat up, shaking hands supporting her on the stone floor. The candle had fallen, its flame extinguished. Now the dungeon was lit only by the emerald-green lights in the skull's eye sockets. Without them she would be lost in darkness.

"Aaaand she's back in the room," Maggoty Skull snickered. "Rise 'n' shine, spotty. First things first, I don't suppose you have a wig on you, do you?"

"I … uh … umm … what have you done with my mother and father?" Mallory croaked.

"Aaaa-*hem*, we're talking about *me*. Pay attention. So: wig. Do you or do you not have one about your person?"

Mallory gritted her teeth, shuffling on to her knees. She

peered into the chest. Green lights stared back up at her, somehow managing to look hopeful. "No," she hissed. "I do not have a wig."

"Well, put that on your to-do list," said the skull. "Right at the top. Wig for Maggoty. *Maaaaggoty*. Maggoty Skull. *Shamone*. Oww. Yeah, baby."

While the skull sang – badly – to itself, Mallory blinked at it.

"Where are my PARENTS?" Her sudden yell echoed around the labyrinth, sending spiders scuttling into the shadows.

The skull sighed, points of green light rolling in their sockets. *"Me,"* it sighed. "Maggoty reminds you: we're talking about me."

"No. We're talking about my mother and father," Mallory insisted. "Where are they?"

"Booo-*ring*," snapped the skull. "Also, how the fuppetty-fup is Maggoty supposed to know where you've misplaced your relatives? Hello? Locked in a box for five hundred years."

Mallory sat back on her heels, slightly less scared. Her eyes narrowed. The skull sounded genuinely confused. Plus, a talking skull was weird, yes, but so far it didn't seem to be the kind of terrifying evil that needed to be sealed in a dungeon with splashy warnings painted on the door.

"Hey, wait," the skull giggled. "Rewind. Maggoty didn't catch your name. Let's get to know the plucky, lucky necromancer who's opened Maggoty's box. Who are you? What's your name and where do you come from, style of thing."

"You know my name," Mallory hissed. "It's Mallory. Mallory Vayle. You called me down here." Making her voice sound spooky, she moaned *"Maaaallory.*

Maaaaaaaallory." Jabbing a finger at the skull, she added, "Ring any bells?"

"Eh?" said Maggoty.

"You did," Mallory insisted.

"Didn't."

"Did."

"Nope. Maggoty most certainly did not. 'Cos – for the second time – locked in a box. Also cursed. Poor Maggoty's spirit can't leave his skull. Can't shout loud enough to be heard outside this dungeon. Do you see, Malls? Ooh, can Maggoty call you Malls? Or how about Malliboo-di-bum-bum?"

"No, you cannot call me Malliboo-di-bum-bum. My mother and father. Where are they?"

"Already said, Maggoty don't know. Are your ears bunged up? Maggoty said, ARE YOUR EARS BLOCKED, Mallsy-Boo?"

"But … but … my parents. Their ghosts. They're *gone.*"

"Oh. Deepest sympathies, and all that. Maggoty wants you to know he is fully sad for your loss at what must be a difficult time. Eat an egg or something. Now, back to important matters: a wig. Blond, don't you think? Maggoty always wanted to be blond."

"Stop jabbering on about wigs. I need to find my parents' ghosts."

"Sheesh, are we still talking about this? Obsessed much? What about me? Why aren't we talking about *meeeeeeeee*?"

Mallory found herself grinding her teeth again. "Answer me, or I'll smash you into the wall."

"Hurtful," said the skull, its eye lights blinking.

"Just. Tell. Me."

"Won't," said Maggoty, sounding sulky.

"Oh, for goodness' sake." Reaching into the chest, Mallory picked the skull up carefully. It weighed more than she expected. With one hand she tossed it in the air thoughtfully, and caught it again.

The skull squealed, "Hurray! Free at last! Maggoty is literally thinking outside the box."

Mallory ignored it. "You say you didn't call me down here," she said. "But someone did. Someone wanted me to find you. Why?"

"Ummmm," Maggoty began, stretching it out for a minute or two. Finally, he admitted in a small voice, "Maggoty doesn't know. Maggoty thought you'd come to bring him a wig."

Mallory put her head to one side. "Seriously?"

"Stranger things have happened."

"No, they haven't," said Mallory, feeling quite confident she was right. "But that's not important. Why did a ghostly voice bring me down here to find you?"

"Ooh, maybe some supernatural force wants you to lift Maggoty's curse! Of course – the curse. You'll help? Wig first, then curse? Oh, Mallory, Mallory Vayle. You're such a tewwific fwiend. You've touched Maggoty's non-existent heart, you big old softy."

"I haven't said I'll lift any curses, and we are *not* friends."

"We'll team up, eh?" crooned the skull. "Maggoty helps Mallory find her ma and pa and Mallory lifts Maggoty's curse? Is that where we're going with this?"

Shaking her head, Mallory said, "No."

The skull ignored her, saying, "Hmmm, it wouldn't be easy. Maggoty's curse is a gaw-blimey curse. Very strong. Very nifty."

Mallory sat back on her ankles, thinking fast. "I don't know anything about lifting curses," she said slowly. "But if you know something that might help me find my parents, I might think about helping."

The skull cackled. "Ooh, bargaining! Haggling!

Maggoty likes your getting-down-to-the-nitty-gritty, no-nonsense style. All right, then. Maggoty helps. Then wig. Then curse lifting."

Without waiting for a reply, the skull went on: "So, what have we discovered so far, Maggoty? Well, Maggoty, in the mystery of the missing parents, Maggoty suspects paranormal forces at work. Ma and Pa Vayle must've been snatched away in some sinister supernatural shenanigans. *Ta-dah*. Another mystery solved, by none other than the splendiferous Mr M. Skull, Esquire. Genius. Applause, applause, applause. Thank you. You've been a lovely audience, *goodnight*." He paused for a second, then finished, "There: *help*. Wig now?"

Mallory rolled her eyes. "You'll have to do better than that. I figured that much all out by myself. *What* supernatural forces?"

The skull answered with a shrug in its voice. "Take your pick. Carrion Castle has a history, see? And a *herstory* too. A *dark* herstory. The place is drenched in wickedness." The skull stopped, then added in a sinister whisper, "Boo boo be doo, *poo*."

"The castle *is* horrid," Mallory said, nodding. "I can feel it. But that doesn't answer my question. Why did the

voice lead me to you?"

"Hmm, that's a mystery still to be solved by the cursed-but-pretty Maggoty Skull and his bumbling sidekick, Mallory Bumcrack."

With a sigh, Mallory poked the skull.

"But if Ma and Pa have gone you'll need Maggoty's help to find 'em. Manky-bottom Mallsy-Boo can start by weaving dark necromancy to—"

Mallory interrupted, "You keep saying that word. What's necromancy?" she asked.

For a few moments, Maggoty gurgled and choked. "Mallory doesn't know what necromancy is. Can you believe what you are hearing, Maggoty Skull?" he gasped. "No, Maggoty Skull, I cannot."

Mallory interrupted. "Could you just answer the question? What's *necromancy*?"

"Aaaargh, there be two things ye must know about necromancy, Mallsy, old chum. First, necromancy is rare. Throughout history only a handful of people have shared its dark, deathly powerses. Necromancers talk to the dead—"

"Oh, is that all?" Mallory interrupted. "We call it 'psychic' these days. I'm not interested in all that spooky

nonsense, though."

"Ha, a lump of cheese wearing dangly earrings could be a psychic. Pff: *psychics.*"

Mallory couldn't help but smile, just a little bit, thinking of her Aunt Lilith. "What makes necromancers different, then?" she asked.

Maggoty sniffed. "Necromancers have awesome powers. Talking to the dead is just the start of it ... and that's *proper* talking to the dead, by the way. None of your crystal ball, table-rapping nonsense. Oh, no. Necromancers command the darkness, rule the creatures of the night, raise things from the dead places. They walk in shadow and much, much more. What makes necromancers different is power. *Dangerous* power. A rama-lama dang dang."

"Umm ... what's the second thing I should know about necromancers?" Mallory asked.

Maggoty's voice sank into a chuckling whisper. "The second thing ye must know about necromancers will shrivel your very soul, Mallory Ballory Vayle." Maggoty paused. "I'm pausing for dramatic effect," he explained.

"Remember, I can break you," Mallory replied.

"Easy, tiger. Maggoty's just trying to create an

atmosphere. No need to make that hideous face."

"I'm not making a face," Mallory replied, blinking.

"Oh," said the skull. "You sure? Oh dear. Poor you. Moving on, then. Where were we?"

"The second thing about necromancy," Mallory prompted through her teeth.

"Oh, yes." The skull's voice dropped even lower. "The second thing ye must know of necromancers," he cackled, "is that *you* – Mallory Vayle – are one of 'em."

Mallory thought about this for a moment. "No, I'm not," she said.

The green points of light in Maggoty's eye sockets flared a little brighter. "Wanna bet?" he chuckled.

CHAPTER 7

Candle forgotten, Mallory used Maggoty's eyes to light her way. They gave the cobwebbed passages an eerie green glow but at least there was no danger of them going out and leaving her in darkness.

"So, we've settled on blond but what about style?" Maggoty cackled. "Hmm, tricksy. Maggoty's leaning towards big and curly. Maybe a fringe swept playfully over one eye socket. What do you think, Boo?"

"I am not a necromancer," Mallory answered.

"It will be a wig that really says, 'Here comes a fabulous skull,'" the skull continued, ignoring her.

"I mean, it sounds horrible," Mallory continued. "Why would anyone want to raise the dead? And why would

anyone want to command the creatures of the night or … or … any of the other things you said."

"Do you think Maggoty should get earrings too?"

"I'm not a necroman— Wait. What? *Earrings*? You haven't got any ears."

"Mallory could glue them to the side of Maggoty's skull. *Bong*. Take the left passage by the statue of the lady with her backside hanging out."

Mallory followed instructions, wrinkling her nose as she walked through yet another cobweb. "Glue-on earrings. Why not?" she murmured. "Nothing else around here makes sense."

"You don't think earrings would be too swishy?"

"Yes… No… I don't care. Look, I'm not a necromancer," Mallory said for the eighteenth time. "I told you I'm not interested in all that spooky stuff."

"Yet here you are, Boo," Maggoty chuckled. "Creeping around an ancient labyrinth beneath a haunted castle in a white nightgown, talking to a cursed skull with your hair all bunged up with cobwebs. Spooky, no? Like something a – *ooh*, I don't know – like something a necromancer might do."

"I'm just…"

The skull sighed. "You're a necromancer, all right. Trust Maggoty on this. For a start, only a necromancer could hear Maggoty's sweet, tinkling voice. Right turn coming up. So, we're agreed that earrings would add that extra splash of elegance. Where do we stand on a jewelled eye patch? Too much?"

Mallory stopped. "This is all too much," she hissed. "Look, all I want is to find my parents' ghosts and to get out of this horrible castle. Why should I trust you to help? Who are you? Why are you cursed? Why are you a ... a *skull*?"

"Yip, yip, yip, we're talking about me again. Maggoty LOVES talking about Maggoty."

"Why are you a skull?" Mallory repeated through her teeth.

"Pff, Maggoty got his head chopped off," sniffed the skull. "It was a disgrace. *Ouches* too. Not kidding. It stings a bit, getting your head cut off."

"Who cut your head off?"

The skull went quiet for a few moments. "Hellysh Spatzl," he whispered eventually, a shiver in his voice. "My old mistress. Magotty used to be her servant. *She* done it."

"Who on Earth is Hellysh Spatzl?" Mallory asked.

"Shh, keep it down, Boo. If her spirit is still haunting this old shack you do *not* want to attract her attention." The skull stopped. Voice sounding like he was being strangled, he went on, "What if it was *her*, talking to you? Oh, whizzers, it might've been her. Umm ... Mallsy Boo, Maggoty wants to go back in the box. Close the door on your way out."

"Will you please hush your nonsense and answer the question?" Mallory huffed.

Lights darted from side to side in Maggoty's eye sockets. Seeming to think the coast was clear, he continued in a low voice. "Might not have been her. Might've been some other ghostie. It's cool. Everything is schmoo. Keep it frosty, Maggoty, old pal. Keep it together."

"Hellysh Spatzl," Mallory reminded him.

Dropping his voice to a low croak, Maggoty said, "Five hundred years ago, Carrion Castle was the home of Hellysh Spatzl. The most powerful necromancer ever to squeeze a still-beating heart in her fist." He paused before going on. "Now you necromancers tend to be a bit on the dark side, but Hellysh ... well ... how can Maggoty put

this? Maggoty doesn't like to be rude. Kind. Generous. Sweet-natured. That's the Maggoty way. Hmm. Let's just say Hellysh was a demented, foul-hearted kitten strangler with dribbling armpits. The type of repulsive hag who'd pick scabs off her own face and make rosy-cheeked children eat them. Also, she had that kind of hair what had fallen out in patches leaving her head looking like someone had scraped out the plughole with a rotten potato. She smelled of wee too. And not just a faint whiff either. Like, a *lot*. And—"

Mallory interrupted. "But you were her servant?"

Maggoty was silent for a few moments before saying, "Yus, well, that maybe wasn't the best employment decision Maggoty ever made but there aren't as many career options as you'd think for gorgeous ne'er-do-wells with a twinkle in their eye and a weakness for mischief. Plus, the pay was good and there were plenty of opportunities for lurking. Who doesn't love a good old lurk, eh?"

"So this Hellysh Spatzl cut your head off. Why?"

Maggoty paused. Mallory got the sense that if he'd had a bottom lip he would have been biting it. After a couple of seconds, he said carefully, "She said it was because

Maggoty was annoying. Can you believe that?"

"Mmm," said Mallory.

"Grave robbing without permission, endless jibber-jabber, general naughtiness. Annoying. That's what she said."

"She said? Were you wrongly accused?"

"*Weeeeeeell,*" said Maggoty, drawing the word out. "Maggoty wouldn't go so far as saying 'wrongly', because he did do all that stuff. Still, cutting Maggoty's head off was a massive overreaction, and – frankly – a right old pain in the neck. Do you see what Maggoty did there? Head cut off? Pain in the neck? Ah ha ha ha HA HA HA. Straight on here."

"I see. What sort of name is Maggoty Skull anyway?" Mallory asked, taking the middle of three passages that ran off a large, vaulted chamber.

"A spiffy name, what drips sweet, sweet mischief," the skull crooned. "But Maggoty Skull wasn't called Maggoty Skull when he was alive."

"What was your name?"

"Something else," said the skull, chuckling. "Something only Maggoty knows. But then he got his head chopped off. Swish. Snip. Splurt. Plonk. Two seconds later,

Hellysh cursed him. The *drama*! It was a whole scene. As the maggots were eating his face after, Maggoty said to himself, 'Well, this is a fine mess you're in, old son.' It changes you as a person, you know – having your head cut off. You feel me?"

"Yes. Yes, it probably would change you," Mallory murmured.

Maggoty Skull ignored her. "Maggoty was upset about it for *weeks* afterwards. Peeved. Put out by the whole ghastly business. Makes you think about what you've done, though. Your life choices and whatnot. Maggoty decided it was time to change his ways, become a better person ... skull."

"You decided to be good?" said Mallory, surprised.

"No, you goose. Maggoty decided to be better at being worse."

"So, you're evil?" Mallory sighed.

"Maggoty prefers 'wicked'. We in the ne'er-do-well community find the word 'evil' quite offensive. 'Sinister' is also acceptable. Your choice. Let's drop the 'E' word, though, shall we?"

Mallory thought about the skull's story for a few minutes. "So, if you're evil – sorry, *wicked* – remind me why I should trust you?"

The skull paused for a moment, then chuckled, the sinister laugh echoing down the stone passage. "You shouldn't trust dear old Maggoty, Mallsy-ballsy-bum-bum-banana," he giggled. "Maggoty is most definitely not to be trusted. He's a naughty, naughty skull. Ba-ba-ba-ba-bad to the bone. Wicked. But if we're talking about wickedness. Is that a word? Wickederociousness? No. Wickederosity? Yeah. If we're talking about wickederosity then you're a flippin' necromancer so Maggoty's gonna have to say ... err, look who's talking, spotty."

"I'm not a necromancer," Mallory repeated.

"You can see ghosts, right? Been seeing the wispy little beggars all your life?"

"I ... err..."

"Maggoty will take that as a big fat YES. You can talk to 'em too?"

"Obviously," Mallory snapped.

"No need to get snippy," sniffed the skull. "Plus, you – Mallsy Wallsy Buttcrack – have an unexplained but powerful darkness rumbling in your belly, hmm? You know you're different. Deep, deep down inside, you know

you were made for the night. Is Maggoty right?"

"I … well…" Mallory mumbled.

"Is Maggoty *right*?" the skull demanded.

"Yes," Mallory admitted in a small voice, forcing the word between lips that were pressed together.

"You're a necromancer all right," Maggoty sniffed. "It's as plain as the nose on my face would be if I had a nose or a face."

"So, I *am* evil, then?" Mallory said, her voice cracking.

"The 'E' word, Mallsy. What have we said about the 'E' word?"

"But I am. I must be. Necromancy. *Death* magic. Will I end up as some horrible, scuttling creature of the night?"

"Let's hope so," chuckled the skull. Maggoty's eyes flared. "It's *sooooo* much fun. Wear a lot of black, that's Maggoty's advice. Goes with everything. Doesn't show the blood stains. Very slimming too."

"But I don't *want* to be a necromancer," said Mallory.

"Boring. Not in the slightest bit interesting. What Maggoty wants to know is Team Maggs n' Mallsy: yes or no? Are we teaming up to solve mysteries, find missing parents, break curses, and fight wickedness – so long as it's other people wickedness and not *us* wickedness? In

short: do we or do we not have a deal?"

"Yes," Mallory whispered. The skull was right: if something supernatural had taken her parents then something else supernatural might help find them. "Yes, if you can help me find my mother and father then I suppose I'll get you a wig and help lift your curse. We have a deal."

"Yay! Maggoty and Mallory, together at last. Oh, girl, we're gonna own it. We're gonna werk it. We're gonna go full necromancer on their bottoms." He paused, then added, "Wig first, though."

The skull fell silent. "Mallory?" a voice called from above. Blinking, Mallory looked up to see her Aunt Lilith silhouetted against sunlight at the top of the steps. She called again: "Mallory? Mallory? Is that you, dear? What on *Earth* are you doing chattering away to yourself down there in all that unspeakable yuck?"

CHAPTER 8

Aunt Lilith stood beneath the chandelier beside a dumpy, middle-aged woman clutching an enormous handbag and swamped by her overcoat and a large, flowery bonnet. Beside her stood a glum-looking ghost wearing a flat cap and a waistcoat. A neat moustache bristled beneath his see-through nose. The ghost, the woman and Aunt Lilith all stared as Mallory clambered out from the dark labyrinth, skull in hand.

She looked from her aunt to the strangers. They goggled back at her.

It was an awkward moment.

"Umm ... hello," Mallory mumbled. "I was just ... err..." She stopped, squinting at her aunt in the light.

While she had been down in the dungeons below
Carrion Castle, morning had arrived. Dim sunlight
streamed through dusty windows high above. Today,
her aunt was wearing a billowing robe of swirling
colours. Her head was wrapped in an equally loud
turban. The outfit made it look like she was dressed in
the flag of a small but outrageously happy country.

"Oh, Mallory," Aunt Lilith said brightly. "You're up.
Wonderful. And you've made a hole in the wall – we'll
talk about that later – plus you're filthy. Your hair is
absolutely *jammed* with cobwebs."

Mallory touched her hair. Aunt Lilith was right, the cobwebs made it feel like a fairground candyfloss. She touched her own face. Her fingertips came away smeared with gack.

"You've made yourself at home, hmm?" her aunt continued, clasping her hands together. "I see you've found a skull too. How *exciting*. Anyone I might know, dear?"

Mallory struggled to find an explanation, and failed. The truth would have to do.

"Errm ... his name is Maggoty," she said eventually, lifting the skull, so her aunt could see it better. "Maggoty Skull. He's ... umm..." She stammered to a stop as she realised where her sentence was going: *he's a wicked, five-hundred-year-old cursed spirit, doomed to spend for ever trapped inside his own skull, and he's going to teach me necromancy so I can find my parents' missing ghosts.* No. She couldn't speak the words out loud. The truth sounded more ridiculous than any lie she could have come up with.

Instead, Mallory glanced behind at the mess she'd made of her aunt's wall. "Umm ... sorry about that," she muttered guiltily, waving Maggoty at the pile of broken

plaster and the dark hole. "I'll clean up."

"Anything valuable down there?" her aunt asked, sounding hopeful.

Mallory shook her head, surprised that her aunt hadn't mentioned the green lights burning in Maggoty's eye sockets. "A few statues. Some old paintings and books, but they've mostly got mushrooms growing on them."

"Can we get on with it?" the dumpy woman beside her aunt interrupted. Her badly fitting false teeth made an odd whistling sound when she spoke. "It's me legs. They're itching again. It's Leonard, isn't it? He's reaching out from beyond the grave and fiddling with me legs."

The ghost beside her rolled his eyes. "I haven't touched her legs," he muttered. "She's wearing cheap stockings again."

Mallory couldn't help snorting quietly. She flashed a glance at the ghost.

His eyes widened. Staring at Mallory, he stammered, "Y-you can *see* me?"

Cursing herself, Mallory lifted one shoulder in a half-hearted shrug. Over the years she had become very good at pretending not to see ghosts. It had been an odd night, she told herself. Her concentration had slipped.

"And hear me?"

Mallory moved her head in a tiny nod.

"Please tell her to let me go," blurted the ghost. "Ever since I died it's been Leonard this, Leonard that. Leonard, Leonard, Leonard. Nine flipping years of it. Couldn't get me out the house fast enough when I was alive but now she won't stop talking to me. It's keeping me stuck…"

His whispery, ghostly voice was drowned out by Aunt Lilith's: "Of course, of course, of course, my dear Mrs Hadley. Together, let us part the flimsy curtain of death once more, shall we?" She paused, then added, "The usual fee, of course."

"Yes, yes, yes," said Mrs Hadley, fiddling with the clasp of her handbag. "Five shillings. I've got the money here."

Cradling the skull in her hands, Mallory raised an eyebrow, shocked. Aunt Lilith couldn't have parted the flimsy curtain of death with an axe. She was charging people for her non-existent talent?

"Gaw, another five shillings," groaned Leonard. "Every week she comes to see that old fraud. It's cost her a fortune."

"You make people *pay*?" Mallory blurted. *"Money?"*

"Just a small contribution," said her aunt smoothly.

Turning back to Mrs Hadley, she continued. "My niece, Mallory. She has the family gift, but – sadly – she is untrained."

"She's lucky to have you as a teacher, then, Mistress Lilith."

Mallory choked. Aunt Lilith patted her on the back, purring, "How kind you are, Mrs Hadley. Please, do come along. Already, my spirit guide, Mr Lozenge, whispers to me. It's a *tickling* in your legs, isn't it?"

"More of a prickling, really."

"*Exactly*. A prickling. Thank you, Mr Lozenge."

Mrs Hadley gasped. "How could you possibly have known that?"

Aunt Lilith held up a hand to stop her. Clutching her forehead, she groaned. "There's a man here."

"Leonard was a man," squeaked Mrs Hadley.

"I'm getting a name... L ... Len ... *Leonard*, is it, Mr Lozenge? Yes, Leonard is here again."

"He's here. He's really here!" Mrs Hadley jiggled from one foot to the other. "Oh, Leonard, you're still coming, every week. Even after all these years. I knew you'd never leave me."

The ghost of Leonard Hadley stuffed his hands in his

ghostly pockets and rolled his eyes.

"Let's make ourselves comfortable in the small séance room and hear what news your dear husband brings from the world of spirit," said Aunt Lilith, turning and sweeping off. "Mallory, please join us. You might learn something." The clacking of her heels echoed through the hall.

"Amazing, isn't she?" whispered Mrs Hadley, winking at Mallory as she bustled past. "Gifted."

Mallory peered around at the cavernous entrance hall, longing – more than anything in the world – to be miles away from its shadows and safely with her mother and father. With a deep breath, she followed her aunt into the gloom. "Heh, heh, heh," Maggoty cackled under her arm. "Let's find out if Maggoty's right and definitely-a-necromancer Mallory is, in fact, wrong, shall we?"

"No," Mallory whispered back. "Let's not."

"Oh, blah, blah, blah," Maggoty replied, giggling. "Blah, blah, blah, blah-de-bum, blah. Work with Maggoty a little, wouldja?"

CHAPTER 9

In the small séance room, Mrs Hadley plumped her wide bottom into a chair. Her eyes glittered with excitement.

"Take a seat, Mallory, dear," said Aunt Lilith, lighting candles.

Nervously, Mallory perched on the edge of a chair, clutching the skull in her lap and letting her eyes wander around the room. Aunt Lilith was good at setting a scene, she had to admit. The small séance parlour was exactly the sort of place where supernatural events unfolded. Candles made the table a mystic island of golden light in the gloom. Silver threads in the tablecloth glinted, tracing out the signs of the zodiac. In the darkness around them, shapes became objects as Mallory's eyes adjusted:

a crystal ball, leather-bound books leaning against each other in heavily carved bookcases. Under a dusty glass dome, a bat skeleton spread bony wings. The room even smelled spooky – a mixture of mould and burned spices.

Aunt Lilith settled into her own chair – a throne of flaking gold paint, padded with faded purple velvet. "First, let's see what the cards can tell us, Mrs Hadley," she said. Taking a thick pack of cards from the table, she began shuffling like a professional gambler, cutting the deck in two and riffling it back together so fast the cards blurred.

Mrs Hadley nodded eagerly. "Are there any spirit people here?" she piped through her whistling teeth. "Knock once for 'yes' and twice for 'no'…"

Aunt Lilith coughed. "It's safer if you leave communicating with the spirits to me, Mrs Hadley," she said. "Tinkering with mystical forces can drive the untrained mind quite, quite mad."

Mallory listened to cards dance in her aunt's hands – cut, riffle, cut, riffle – while her aunt breathed deeply, eyelids fluttering while she muttered to herself: "Mr Lozenge, my dear guide, we have one among us who seeks to communicate with the spirit of Leonard Hadley.

I beg you, Mr Lozenge, lead him even unto this *dismal* earthly place. Let him speak from beyond the grave."

Mallory jumped as a card sprang out of the deck and fluttered on to the table.

"Thank you, Mr Lozenge," said Aunt Lilith, in a low voice. "A message from your husband, I think, Mrs Hadley."

Leonard's ghost muttered something rude.

Leaning forward, Aunt Lilith flipped the card over. "Ah, of course. The Ace of Cats. Just as I was expecting. You see here, Mrs Hadley, the woman with the cat at her feet."

"Ooh, the cat was sick on the carpet this morning," said Mrs Hadley, peering at the card. "Is it bad news for Truffles?"

"Please, Mrs Hadley, don't interrupt," Aunt Lilith hissed, holding up a hand. "Ahh, I see it now. Yes. Yes, Mr Lozenge. He's drawing my attention to the way the cat is rubbing against the woman's legs."

"Leonard!" gasped Mrs Hadley. "It *is* him, touching me legs."

"Five shillings for this rubbish," huffed the ghost of Leonard Hadley. "She could've bought herself some decent stockings."

Mallory bit her bottom lip. Leonard Hadley was right. Her Aunt Lilith was cheating a poor, sad woman who missed her husband.

"This is just tragic," giggled Maggoty, echoing Mallory's thoughts. "What are you waiting for, Boo? Show the old muffins what you can do."

"Shut up. They'll hear you," Mallory hissed from the corner of her mouth.

"Silly, silly Mallory," the skull giggled. "Maggoty said only a necromancer could hear his voice. Also, he said he'd teach you new tricks. Maggoty learned a thing or two watching Hellysh so welcome to the Maggoty Skull School of the Supernatural."

"I can't," Mallory hissed.

"If you want to find Mummy and Daddy you can," tittered Maggoty.

Aunt Lilith peered at Mallory. "Are you all right, dear?" she asked. "You seem to be mumbling to yourself again."

"I … ahh … talk to myself sometimes," Mallory replied.

"You *are* a peculiar girl," said her aunt. "But if you don't mind, Aunty Lilith is trying to connect with the world of spirit, hmm?"

"Sorry," Mallory murmured. "Please. Carry on."

Another card flew from the deck. This one showed a crowned woman with a big smile. For some reason she

was holding what looked like a toilet brush.

The card was upside down.

"The Queen of Teeth," Aunt Lilith said. "In the reversed position. Hmm. A powerful message. Thank you, Mr Lozenge. Tell me, Mrs Hadley, are you having any dental problems?"

"Oooh, yes, I have been having some difficulties in that area," whistled Mrs Hadley, false teeth rattling in her head. "It *must* be Leonard. He was always going on about the importance of good dentistry."

The ghost of her husband groaned. "She's being taken for a ride: conned, cheated. It's a disgrace."

Mallory nodded. Leonard Hadley was right – her aunt was a complete fraud. It *was* a disgrace.

Without thinking, Mallory looked across the table into Mrs Hadley's eyes and growled, "Leonard thinks this is a waste of money."

"*Yessssssss,*" screeched Maggoty. "Now we're getting somewhere."

CHAPTER 10

Blinking, Aunt Lilith said, "Sorry, Mallory dear, did you say something?"

Mallory sat up straighter. "I said, you're making it up as you go along. Leonard says so too. He's standing right behind you, by the way, Mrs Hadley."

Mrs Hadley glanced nervously over her shoulder. Seeing nothing, she turned back with a shrug.

Aunt Lilith turned pale. "I'm so sorry, Mrs Hadley," she said. "My niece is having a difficult time, aren't you, darling? Sadly, her parents recently passed into the world of spirit. Perhaps, Mallory, you should wait outside..."

"No, I don't think I will," Mallory snapped. "Leonard wants you to know that he hasn't touched your legs, you're just wearing cheap stockings…"

"*Mallory!*"

Mallory shook her head. "No," she said. "I *won't* be quiet. You're conning this woman. But *I* can speak to Leonard…"

"How *dare* you, Mallory," snapped Aunt Lilith. "I've spent my entire life training and—"

"And you *still* have no psychic talent," Mallory finished for her.

Aunt Lilith gasped, clutching her heart.

Leonard Hadley punched the air behind his wife. "Yes," he shouted. "Tell Daisy I'm—"

"This *cannot* be suffered," squealed her aunt. "Mr Lozenge—"

"—doesn't exist," Mallory snapped, folding her arms. Turning her head to Mrs Hadley, she continued. "Leonard really does want to speak to you. Normally, I don't talk to ghosts but he seems like a nice man and it's important, I think."

"Mr Lozenge," wailed her aunt, lifting her arms to the ceiling. "An evil spirit has possessed my niece. Drive it out so that we may return to our mystical business in peace."

Mallory snorted. "I'm not possessed," she said calmly.

"Mrs Hadley, I really can speak to Leonard."

"A twig of a girl like you?" sniffed Daisy Hadley. "Leave it to your aunt, love. She's the expert."

"Fine, then." Mallory shrugged. "Throw your money away."

"Her full name is Daisy *Spatula* Hadley," said Leonard, his voice urgent. "Her old mum wasn't very bright. She thought 'Spatula' was a girl's name. Daisy never tells anyone."

Mallory nodded. "Leonard says your middle name is Spatula," she repeated.

Mrs Hadley squawked. Her chair flew backwards. She crashed into the floor, her legs sticking up in the air. She was, Mallory noticed, wearing cheap stockings.

Her aunt gawped. Mrs Hadley scrabbled on the floor. Her eyes appeared over the edge of the table, filled with terror. *"Leonard?"* she rasped.

Leonard was talking fast now. Mallory waved him into silence so she could catch up. "He says cheese makes you fart something dreadful. You nearly missed your wedding because you accidentally locked yourself in the toilet. You've got a rash in your right armpit. It's been itching lately. You're a bit worried about it but you haven't told

anyone. Do you believe I can speak to him now?"

White-faced and trembling, Daisy Hadley nodded.

"Good."

"What messages do you bring from the beyond, Leonard?" squeaked Mrs Hadley in a wobbly voice. "Is Truffles going to be all right? Should I take him to the vet?"

"Leonard says he doesn't give a monkey's bum about your mangy cat," said Mallory, tilting her head to listen as the ghost gabbled quickly.

"Oooh, is he going to reveal mystic knowledge beyond our pitiful human understanding, then?" asked Mrs Hadley, her voice trembling with awe.

"No," said Mallory firmly. "His first message is that you can stuff all this hokey-pokey, parting-the-curtains-of-death nonsense. He says, would you please let him go? He's supposed to be resting in peace and all this séance stuff is rubbish. My aunt has been swindling you for years."

Aunt Lilith's jaw dropped another inch or two. She began making odd meeping noises.

"Maggoty is mildly enjoying this, Mallsy," the skull in her lap interrupted. "But just so you know, it is all a bit

tea leaves. As a necromancer, you do have choices here. Option one: melt everyone's brain. Hellysh used to do that to people all the time. Show them stuff what human eyes are not supposed to see. *Weird* stuff. It'd be a right laugh and by the time you finished scrambling their minds they'll all think they're a pancake named Jeffrey."

Mallory ignored him, and continued, "Until you stop hanging on to Leonard, talking to him all the time, you're both stuck. Leonard can't move on to wherever it is you're supposed to go when you die and you're wasting your life wishing he was still alive. He says it's been nine years. Time you stopped moping and got on with things. Let him be dead. Yes?"

Mrs Hadley yelped. "But ... but... *Leonard*..." she started.

"Pwease, pwease, pwease, pwease, pwease do brain melting. For sweet widdle Maggoty."

Once again, Mallory ignored him. She held up a hand to stop Mrs Hadley's babbling. "Leonard is still talking. He says he was saving up to buy a little cottage by the seaside when he retired. It was going to be a surprise. There's a bank book in the shed, under a box of old paint. There's almost five hundred pounds in a secret

account." Again, Mallory paused. "He says you're not dead yet so get yourself a new set of teeth and have some fun."

"Five *hundred* pounds?"

Mallory nodded. Speaking more slowly now, she said in a kinder voice, "He says you should be able to have a good old knees-up with that, eh, Mopsy?"

"He always called me 'Mopsy.'" Tears rolled down Daisy Hadley's face. "But how can I let him go when I miss him so much?"

"This is boring. Like total dullingtons. Yawnsville. Use your necromancy, Boo," Maggoty crooned. "Give 'em a show. Just a little drop of necromancer juice. Let Maggoty guide you. You're going to have to anyway. Might as well make a start."

"Will you shut up?" Mallory hissed under her breath.

"Nope. Not even a little bit. Use the darkness within. The ghastly powerses of the nether regions. Show them the spirit world. Show Maggoty."

"I ... don't ... think ... I..."

"Do it, Boo," the skull ranted. "Scare the knickers off the old twazzocks. Make them poop their own kidneys."

Up until now everything had been quite weird.

It now got about sixteen and a half times weirder. A wave of darkness rolled through Mallory. No longer thinking straight, or even thinking at all, she felt herself lean across the table. Closing her eyes, she felt a curling vine of shadow curl up from her stomach, flowing down her arm. A darkly purple spark of strange magic crackled from her fingertips into the ghost.

Her aunt croaked like a dying frog and fell back in her chair.

Mrs Hadley screamed.

Mallory opened her eyes to see Mrs Hadley staring straight into her dead husband's face, her mouth an astonished 'O'.

Leonard Hadley looked more – Mallory felt her own jaw sag – solid. He was still wispy around the edges – obviously a ghost – but with a touch she had somehow dragged him partway back into the world of the living.

He could be seen.

"And the crowd goes wild," shrieked the skull. "The judges scores are in and we've got tens, tens, tens. To absolutely no one's surprise Maggoty was right and Mallory was wrong. She's a necromancer all right. And what's more, she's a natural. Cheers. Fireworks.

Glitter. Dancers in spangly outfits. Fabulous work. Bravo. *Bravissimo.*"

Leonard's hand reached out to his wife. Trembling, Daisy Hadley lifted her own hand. Their fingers twined. "Life is for living, Mopsy," Leonard said softly. "You'll be fine. Let me go. *Please* let me go."

He could be heard too.

"I will, Lenny. I will," wept his wife.

"Say it. Say you release me."

"I ... I ... release you, love."

"That's my girl." Leonard winked. "Wherever it is we end up, I'll be waiting. But it's all right if you make me wait a long, long time."

Leonard's ghost was already fading. Whatever power Mallory had given it didn't last long. Mallory watched as his spirit slipped away. "I love you, Mopsy," he said, his voice faint. "Goodbye for now. Oh, and get that rash checked, you daft old trout."

The spirit vanished. Mallory slumped back in her chair. Looking into the stunned, bloodless face of her aunt, she whispered, "Not a word. I do not want to hear a single word. I've had a really, *really* odd night and I want to go to my room. Nod if you understand."

Her aunt nodded. She cleared her throat. "Yes ... yes, of course," she said in a high-pitched voice. "Yes ... thank you, Mallory. Erm ... that will be five shillings then, Mrs Hadley."

Too dazed to argue, Mrs Hadly dropped coins into Aunt Lilith's outstretched palm.

Mallory stood, clutching the still-giggling skull, which was now mimicking her voice, "'I'm not a necromancer, Maggoty. Ooh, no. I'm just a dull, spotty little girl.' Ha ha ha HA HA! Told you, you're a necromancer. Didn't Maggoty say? Yes, Maggoty did."

"Please shut up," Mallory begged, under her breath.

"But let's try a *leeeeetle* bit harder next time, huh?" Maggoty wittered. "Helping lost souls move on is a bit namby-pamby, wet-knickers necromancing for Maggoty. Brain-melting visions would've been *waaaay* better. Spooks with flaps of skin hanging off their fingers and whatnot. Mallsy-bum? Hey, Mallsy? Aren't you forgetting something?"

Mallory sighed – cold, hungry and suddenly so tired she could cry. "Aunt Lilith," she said, interrupting the skull's chatter. "Do you happen to have a wig?"

CHAPTER 11

Night had fallen once more. Outside, clouds had tangled in the city's towers and spires and were spitting hail at the window. Having slept through the day, Mallory was surprised to find that she felt... She shook her head. *Better* was the wrong word. Worry about her vanished parents gnawed at her, and the horrible sense of evil that drenched Carrion Castle *still* drenched Carrion Castle. Even without the atmosphere of cold, slimy evil, her room would be chilly and damp. There was mouse poo in the fireplace and grimy cobwebs stretched from peeling walls to the stained ceiling. The four-poster bed was buckled, sagging and smelly. In one corner stood the sort of wardrobe bright-eyed children might walk

into, only to find themselves in a strange fantasy land, though this wardrobe could only lead to a world where bad-tempered gnomes punched them in the knees and stole their wallets.

On top of all that, the news that she was some sort of dreadful, dark wizard was still upsetting. But the soft moonlight that filtered through her window was curiously soothing, and at least she had someone to talk to even if it was a massively annoying, jibber-jabbering skull. She wasn't feeling better, she decided, but somewhere deep inside she could feel a tiny twinge of relief. Maggoty might be odd – *very* odd, she corrected herself – but when it came right down to it, so was she. For the first time in her life she could talk to someone who might, just might, help her understand a part of herself she had been ignoring for as long as she could remember. Even her parents had done their best to ignore her strange talent and it was never talked about around the family dinner table.

Quickly, she scraped bread around the cold remains of what might have been soup that she'd found outside her door. Pushing the empty bowl away, Mallory lay on her stomach across the end of her bed and propped her chin in her hands, watching the skull on the dressing table.

"Wig," Maggoty Skull crooned, points of light within his eye sockets glowing as he stared into the cracked mirror on the dressing table, a candle to either side lighting him like an actor preparing to go onstage. "Wiggy wiggy wig wig."

Mallory coughed impatiently. The wig Aunt Lilith had unearthed from a room crammed with old junk was tall, curled and two hundred years out of fashion; more white than blond and more filthy than white. Large patches of hair had fallen out. It was well past scruffy and had entered health hazard territory.

"Maggoty," she said.

"Not now," croaked the skull. "Maggoty is having a moment. This wig. It's ... it's ... everything. Maggoty. Looks. *Stunning*."

"You look like a diseased sheep is squatting on your head."

The skull ignored her. "Not many people could wear a wig like this," he murmured. "But on Maggoty it looks divine."

Mallory rolled her eyes.

"What is this vision of gorgeousness before us?" the skull continued. "Why it's only a beautifully bewigged Maggoty Skull. Has anyone ever seen such perfection?" A dead mouse dropped out of the wig. "Gosh darn it," Mallory heard him whisper. "You look amazing, Maggoty. Not just spiffy, but really, *really* smashing."

"I got you a wig. Your turn to help me," Mallory snapped.

The skull's jaw clattered on the dusty surface of the dressing table. Like a cheap wind-up toy, Maggoty spun away from the mirror to face Mallory. The top-heavy wig sagged over one eye socket. "Beheaded," he sniffed. "Five hundred years locked in a dark box, all alone. *Excuuuuse*

Maggoty for taking a moment."

Mallory got to her feet and crossed the floor. Setting the skull's wig straight and arranging a few curls to fall shyly over an eye socket, she wiped her hands on her skirts. In a gentler voice, she said, "I have to find my parents and get out of this horrible castle. Can you *please* pay attention? You said something supernatural must have taken them."

"Yes, yes, yes, yes, yes," replied the skull, eye sockets flaring. "Carrion Castle is chock-a-block with haunty folk. Headless horsemen, grey ladies, white ladies, greyish-white ladies, poltergeists and sinister spirits – we got the lot. Why don't you send your shadow out to ask them if they've seen Ma and Pa? Maggoty will stay here and gaze upon the gorgeous, gorgeous loveliness of wig."

"My shadow?" Mallory's forehead wrinkled. "What? What are you on about now?"

"You don't know about shadow walking?" the skull gasped. "Stamp on Maggoty's snails, Mallsy, Maggoty knew you were utterly and completely useless. Not just a little bit rubbish but a whole great—"

"Were you making a point?"

"Maggoty's point is: shadow walking. Any kind of shadow play is baby stuff! You are a flippin' necromancer.

The shadows are yours. You belong to them. They belong to you. Shadow is yours to command, type of thing. Feel the darkness. Walk among it."

"I'm not a necro—" Mallory bit her tongue. There was no point lying to herself. Instead, she turned her attention to the dark corners of the room, and immediately felt a connection. The darkness inside her shifted, reaching out to the shadows. The skull was right. She could … touch the shadows … yes … *shape* them…

Mallory's eyes widened. On the wall opposite, a small patch of darkness shaped like a pony broke away. Tossing its mane it cantered across the stained wallpaper on hooves of night.

"Ponies!" shrieked the skull in disgust.

The shadow-pony disappeared.

"I *like* ponies," said Mallory, refusing to feel ashamed.

"What sort of child of the night likes ponies?" Maggoty huffed. "Ri-donk-ulous. What you want is gruesome body parts…"

"Will you please stop babbling and help? Even if I could use my shadow to explore, I don't know this castle. *You* do. So, stop admiring yourself and come with me."

Green points of light twinkled. "Ahh, Maggoty gets

it now," the skull snickered. "Mallsy-ballsy-bumpkin cannot bear to be parted from sweet, adorable Maggoty. It's a nightmarish obsession, isn't it, Boo? A moment away from Maggoty feels like a thousand lifetimes of pain and torture? Doesn't it? Doesn't it?"

"For goodness' sake." Mallory rolled her eyes and picked up the skull. Outside, the moon sailed on seas of cloud over the mismatched roofs. Wind moaned through the castle's broken stones.

"Oi, watch the wig!"

Tucking Maggoty under her arm, Mallory walked to the door and out into the creeping darkness of Carrion Castle.

CHAPTER 12

"Well, this is a surprise," whispered Maggoty an hour later. "Where did all the ghosties go? Maggoty is shocked and nonplussed. Discombobulated. Not even a tiny bit bobulated."

Mallory nodded. It *was* strange. She had been expecting the draughty passages and forgotten rooms of Carrion Castle to be crawling with spirits. From outside, the crumbling fortress looked like a ghost's idea of the perfect holiday spot. It was old – older even than Mallory had thought. Newer parts of the castle had been built over ancient parts. Rooms had been abandoned and ceilings left to collapse. After an hour of walking through empty passages where leaves had blown in through broken windows, Mallory and Maggoty had found only spiders, rats and the ever-present stain of gloom. The entire castle groaned under the weight of a sinister presence but there was not a ghost to be found anywhere: not a single spirit who might be able to give a clue about what had happened to her parents.

"I don't understand," Mallory whispered back. "Where are they all? The castle is haunted. There's something here. Something awful. I can feel it. The whole place reeks of evil."

"The 'E' word, Boo," Maggoty hissed.

Mallory shook her head. "It's the only way to describe it. It feels like the castle is drenched in horror."

"Oh dear, oh dear, oh dear," muttered the skull. "Would it, by any chance, feel like the sort of grisly, brain-twisting horror that might – for example – chop off the delightful head of a totally innocent bystander who'd done nothing wrong at all?"

"Yes," Mallory told him. "Very much exactly like that."

"Gulp," whispered Maggoty to himself. "Maggoty was afraid of this. But of course she would be haunting the place. *Pff*, she always was a dark-spirit-what-lurks-in-the-attic waiting to happen. She wouldn't have let a little thing

like death force her out of her own castle. And if it *is* her then it's no surprise the other ghosties have all scarpered. Who'd want to be within a bezillion miles of *her*? Eeek, that means it *was* her what led you to Maggoty's box. But *why*, Boo? That's the question on the lips of everyone who has lips."

"Who? What are you talking about?" Mallory whispered back.

"*Hellysh*, of course," Maggoty hissed in a voice so low Mallory could barely hear it. "Don't you listen? Hellysh Spatzl. The bent-kneed, pigeon-infested, demon-bottom-prodding, poisonous, gristle-hearted, head-cutter-offer what cursed poor, poor Maggoty and turned him into this wretched-but-pretty skull you see before you today."

On the edge of hearing, Mallory heard spiteful cackling in the distance. Wind threw hail at the windows. A cold draught fluttered the candle she was holding. Lightning flashed the room into stark black and white for an instant. Maggoty Skull groaned. "Umm, Boo?" he whimpered. "If Hellysh Spatzl is behind Ma and Pa's strange disappearance then Maggoty strongly – *very* strongly – suggests we leave Carrion Castle right now and start a new life in far-off parts disguised as walruses."

"What would the ghost of an old necromancer want with my parents?" Mallory asked.

"Don't know, don't care," hissed the skull. "Best forget about 'em. We'll miss them. Of course we will. But we wish them well in their new career as captives of history's most vile necromancer. Still, never mind. A new life beckons. Bright side: Maggoty will look super-cute with a big droopy walrus moustache."

"We're not leaving," Mallory told him, her voice firmer than her knees felt. "Not without my ma and da. Where do we find this Hellysh Satchel?"

"*Spatzl*. Errrm ... are you still not listening? We don't *find* her. We run *away* from her. And if we were trying to find her we *definitely* would not look in her old tower," said Maggoty. The skull shook under Mallory's arm. "Maggoty and Mallory definitely, *totally* wouldn't want to go up there."

"Her tower," said Mallory. "Which way?"

The tower leaned over a forgotten, overgrown courtyard where the thorns of skeletal trees clawed at Mallory's skirts. Its windows were little more than slits. Roots had burrowed through the walls. The entrance was not exactly secret but would have been impossible to find behind thick curtains of ivy if Maggoty had not – after a five-minute argument – pointed it out.

Thunder rocked the sky. Rain pattered on Mallory's shoulders.

"Creepy," Mallory murmured, lifting her wet face to gaze at the battlements high above.

"Pff," squeaked Maggoty, sounding petrified. "You ain't seen nuthin' yet."

Hand trembling, Mallory pushed a door open. Rusty hinges squealed. "Where does this go?" she murmured, lifting the heavily wigged skull so his eyes illuminated a spiral staircase, twisting up into darkness.

"It leads to Hellysh's private room," Maggoty squeaked. "The very spot Maggoty met his cruel fate. The place we'll find her. Still time to run away. Walruses, yes? It's a good life as a walrus."

Heart drumming, Mallory ignored him and climbed into darkness, one hand on the slimy, crumbling wall to steady herself, the other lifting the skull to light her way. Breathing in ragged pants, she climbed in circles, footsteps muffled by dust.

"Picture, if you will, the scene," Maggoty murmured. "It's five hundred years ago. Hellysh Spatzl walks these very stairs, with Maggoty's head swinging by the hair from her grip. Blood is still dripping from the grisly stump of his neck."

Mallory glanced down. The steps were spotted and

stained. "Do you have to tell this story *now*?" she muttered.

Wind moaned around the broken tower. Below, the door slammed shut.

The skull took no notice, and continued: "Maggoty was *not* having a good day, but what's this? It was about to get much, *much* worse. In a swirl of *gharrrstly* magicks, Maggoty's spirit is dragged back from death and sealed – *entombed* – inside his own head. His last glimpse of the outside world as the lid comes down on the box. Maggoty rolls, helpless, tumbling inside as it's roughly carried down, down, down, deep underground. A door slams. The sound of chains. And hammering. Maggots chewing Maggoty's face. After that, silence. Nothing but silence. Five hundred years of silence."

The tower juddered and groaned.

Maggoty sniffed. "And *someone* – no names – couldn't give Maggoty a moment to enjoy his new wig," he finished.

"Are you still going on about that?" Mallory stopped as the stairs ended. She stepped into the ancient room at the top of the tower. Floorboards groaned beneath her feet. Holding up the skull, the green lights of Maggoty's eyes fell on bats, hanging from the ceiling. Disturbed,

they chittered around the room before leaving through a crack in the wall, fluttering into the storm outside.

Unable to help herself, Mallory yelped.

"Sheesh," squeaked the skull. "It's *bats*. You are a *terrible* child of the night."

Mallory bit back a rude reply. Holding Maggoty high, she flashed his torch eyes around the room. Rags fluttered in the narrow windows. *"Bones,"* she gasped, horrified. A large desk stood in one corner, its legs made from human leg bones. A chandelier made of more bones hung lopsidedly from the ceiling. Skeletal hands had been fixed to every wall, a few holding ancient candle stubs. Everywhere she looked bones had been used to decorate Hellysh Spatzl's private chamber.

Voice squeaking with fear, Maggoty said, "She always did have a thing about bones. Can we go now?"

"In a moment," Mallory hissed, turning him this way

and that to illuminate the circular room. Her shoulders sagged in relief. "No ghosts," she hissed. "She's not here."

A painting fell from the wall, crashing to the floor. Mallory spun, flashing Maggoty's eyes at the portrait. Time and mould had ruined it but it was still possible to make out a haughty young woman with dark hair and a cold smile. One heavily jewelled hand held the strings to a puppet: a skeletal figure in black robes and holding a scythe. The other held a human skull.

"That was painted when she was young," squeaked Maggoty. "Before Maggoty's time. As she got deeper into the necromancy she really let herself go. Went full raggedy crone." He sniffed. "It's a look, Maggoty supposes, if feeding princesses poisoned apples is your vibe."

Mallory barely heard him. She was frozen, eyes fixed on the portrait. Somehow – by some tragic quirk of fate or cosmic accident – she shared Hellysh Spatzl's dark power. How? *Why?* And did that mean she shared this young Hellysh's future too? Was she destined to become a creepy hag whose idea of interior design was nailing skeletons to the wall?

Mallory ground her teeth together, promising herself that she would find her parents, leave Carrion Castle and

never, ever use necromancy again. She might never be truly normal but she could at least pretend.

"*Maaaallloreeee.*"

"What was that?" Mallory gasped, spinning and, flashing Maggoty's eyes around the tower room. There was nothing there, but the presence that had been watching Mallory since she had arrived at Carrion Castle was close now. She could feel it oozing into the room, bringing a cold, stinking chill with it. Once again she was reminded of the faint but stomach-twisting presence she'd felt on Gibbett Bridge. Every inch of her skin prickled with goosebumps.

"*Maallory.*"

With a frightened eep, Mallory spun on the spot again. The shadow of a ragged, hooded figure flitted across the wall, always behind her, unseen.

"Get back," Mallory commanded.

Her voice echoed around the room, transformed and speaking words Mallory had not spoken but which whispered with the power of necromancy. "Back ... get back ... foul spirit..."

Words that came straight from the well of dark power deep within Mallory.

Words that nothing made of spirit could ignore.

The shadow jerked as if tugged by an invisible hook. A snarl sounded beneath the hood.

"Yay, Mallsy-Ballsy-di-bum-bum used The *Voice*!" the skull squeaked in excitement. "The Voice!" he crooned. "Your ack-chew-al, Secret Voice of Necromancy. That's intermediate level stuff, that is. You go, girl."

Mallory ignored him. Whirling, she flashed Maggoty's eye sockets around the room.

The shadow had melted away.

"Put a bit more oomph into it, though, eh, Boo?"

Once again, Mallory paid the skull no attention. She twisted on the spot sensing the stomach-churning presense of Hellysh Spatzl growing stronger again already.

"Maallorrrrrrry." The voice sounded angry now.

Mallory whirled again to see nothing.

"Something's not right here, Mallsy," squeaked the skull.

"Really?" Mallory replied, her voice equally high-pitched. "What makes you think that?"

Ignoring the sarcasm, Maggoty hissed, "Where's the ghost, eh?"

The hunched figure, made of darkness, crossed the wall behind Mallory, disappearing into shadow again as she turned, reappearing out of sight on the opposite wall.

"*Maaallorrrryyyyyyy.*"

"Enough," Mallory yelped through chattering teeth. She turned on shaking legs to see nothing but the rags of curtains blowing at empty windows. "Where are my parents?"

Her only reply was a distant cackle.

"She was always like this," sighed Maggoty. "Hissing, cackling, wheezing. It's very off-putting."

"You were her servant," Mallory whispered.

"Yes, well, like Maggoty said there weren't many job opportunities back then," babbled the skull, teeth chattering. "Oh, Maggoty was offered a position in the pig muck industry, but he would've had to start at the bottom. And when Maggoty says 'bottom' he really means it."

The shadow crept around the walls, flickering on the very edge of Mallory's sight and disappearing whenever she turned her head to look. Limping, it shuffled around the walls, inspecting her, always staying just out of sight. "*Necromancccerr,*" it said unexpectedly.

"Yes," Mallory replied through gritted teeth, holding Maggoty up and flashing his eye sockets around the room. "At least, the skull seems to think so. Where are my parents? Tell me."

Once again, Mallory's voice rippled with strange echoes – *"Tell me ... me ... me..."*

"Now you're getting it," chirped Maggoty.

Writhing angrily, the shadow behind her grew, looming over Mallory and creeping across the crumbling stone ceiling. "They *ssssuffer*," it said.

Gulping, Mallory whirled.

The shadow had gone.

Mallory heard her mother's voice, coming from far away: "Mallory. She wants you to bring her back to life. Don't. Whatever you do, don't. Get out. Get out *now...*"

Silence. Then her father was speaking. "Mallory, we lov—"

Furious, Mallory whipped round, seeing nothing. "Give them back," she screamed.

"Give them ... give them ... give them ... foul shade..."

Too angry and frightened to pay any attention to the strange fizzing in her stomach and the way the darkness within seemed to twist through her words, Mallory spun

again, trying to see the ghost that had stolen her parents. Instead, all she heard was the sound of the same cackling voice saying, *"No."*

"What do you want?" Mallory yelled. "You want me to bring you back to life? I can't. I don't know how and even if I did I…"

"Book," whispered Hellysh Spatzl's voice. *"Diary.* The traitor. Matthew … help."

"Eh? What now?" Mallory frowned. "Who's Matthew?"

"Ummm," squeaked the skull in her hand. "She might, in fact, be talking about Maggoty."

Mallory jerked the skull down until its eye sockets were looking into her own from inches away. "You!" she hissed. "You're part of this! That's why you offered to help me."

"Umm … no," yelped the skull. "You've got it all wrong, Boo. Maggoty was just sitting in his box minding his own business and—"

"Matthew will teeeach…" Hellysh interrupted. "As I planned. Find book… Waited. Waited. *Necromanccccer.* Power of the night…"

Shadow flitted across the wall at Mallory's back.

"Knowledge … a trade … bring me back. Trade…"

"A trade? What are you talking about now?" Mallory demanded, her eyes darting around the room and seeing nothing.

Maggoty interrupted. "Uh … Boo?" he squeaked quietly.

"What?"

"Maggoty thinks he knows."

Mallory glared into the skull's glowing eye sockets. "Tell me."

Seeing the look on Mallory's face, the skull said hurriedly, "She used to have a book. A diary. Wrote everything in it. 'Got up at dusk, spawned evil, bed before dawn.' That sort of thing. But also all her nasty tricks and magicks. *Woo.* That's why she led you to Maggoty's box. Maggoty knows her secrets. There's something written in her book that a necromancer like Boo can use to bring her back to life. With Maggoty's help."

"I see," Mallory breathed, aghast at the horror of it. "What about this trade?"

Maggoty paused, then went on, sounding even more scared. "If … if … you performed Hellysh's dark rituals to bring her back from the dead, you'd have to follow her icky step-by-step guide to raising creatures from the

actual grave, wouldn't you?"

"Meaning..." the disembodied voice of Hellysh Spatzl prompted.

"Meaning, I'd know how to do it." Mallory's eyes widened. "And I could do it again? Bring other spirits back to life?"

"Ker-*chingg*. The bunny drops," Maggoty whispered. "*Exakkerly*. That's the trade. You bring her back and then you work the ritual again. Another *two* times, maybe."

Mallory gasped. Her jaw fell towards the floor.

The shadow loomed behind her, chuckling.

"You're telling me I could bring my mother and father back from the dead?" Mallory gurgled.

"That's what she's offering," Maggoty squeaked. "But, Mallsy-bum, no. You can't. You just can't..."

Mallory shook her head, ignoring him. "She planned everything. It was *her*," she whispered, twisting her head to try and catch a glimpse of the invisible Hellysh. "Somehow – I don't know how – she knew I was a necromancer too. Somehow she found me, and led me to you. She showed me the door to the dungeons. She..." Mallory stopped and gasped, remembering the faint stench of evil on Gibbett Bridge. "She frightened the

horses and drove them off the bridge. She's been waiting for another necromancer and when one arrived she made sure I'd be just where she wanted me. She killed my parents, then took them away from me. So she could blackmail another necromancer into bringing her back."

"*Yesss,*" said the voice from the shadows.

Mallory stopped, her mind whirling. How far back did Hellysh's plan go? Her aunt had said she had inherited Carrion Castle under mysterious circumstances. Had Hellysh Spatzl been behind that too? It was a staggering achievement, especially for a ghost. A long, *long* way from staring out of windows and groaning.

"*How?*" Mallory whispered. "How did you know? How did you do it all? And *why*? Why not just be dead and leave everyone in peace?"

"Uh uh ahh. No cluessss. Hellysh's secretsssesss," cackled the shadow. There was spite in her voice, but it sounded weaker now, as if Hellysh was struggling to remain present.

Mallory's free hands curled into a fist, fingernails cutting into the skin of her palm. When she spoke, her voice was as cold and hard as avalanches. "It doesn't matter. All that matters is you have me exactly where you

want me. There's nothing I can do, is there? If I don't do what you say I'll never see my parents again. Maggoty was right. You are *vile*."

Shadow writhed on the wall behind her. *"Yessss,"* giggled the voice of Hellysh Spatzl. "How kind of you to noticcce."

"Well, ha ha," crowed Maggoty. "Maggoty's seen the flaw in your so-called plan! No more training. *Refusio*. Mallory learns nothing else from Maggoty Skull. That'll shove a turnip up your so-called plans, won't it?"

"You will, though, Maggoty," said Mallory quietly. "You will help me. Because if you don't it's bye-bye wig and back in the box for ever. No one will ever find you again."

"Eh? Eh? What's this? Who said anything about going back in the box? Who's going to stuff poor Maggoty back in the box?"

"Me," said Mallory simply.

"You wouldn't, Boo! Not dear old Maggoty!"

"My parents are coming back," Mallory whispered. "All of this… They died because of me … and I will make everything right again. I will bring them back. Whatever the cost. Where is this book?"

"The *pssssychic*," hissed the strange shadow, its voice fading now. "It'sss gone... Sold..."

"Aunt Lilith," said Mallory, lifting her head. "She sold it?"

"*Yesssss.*"

Thunder shook the castle. The shadow of Hellysh Spatzl flickered across the wall and vanished. The air inside her tower suddenly felt fresher.

"Yeah, that's right: get lost," jeered Maggoty Skull. "Huh, that showed you, Hellysh Spatzl, ya rotted bum stain. Brilliant, Boo. You had her going there, eh? You even had Maggoty going for a minute! Heh. She really thought you'd bring her back to life. Like *whaaaat*? As if. Ha ha ha HA HA. Plonker. She'll eat her own scabby underwear when she finds out you were just tweaking her oojamawhatsits and squeezing her faddubadubs. Malls? Mallsy? Boo? You were tweaking her oojamawhatsits and squeezing her faddubadubs, right?

"*Boo?*"

CHAPTER 13

Mallory woke from blanket-twisting dreams with a shiver. Opening her eyes, she blinked away the tatters of nightmare: the castle alone in a forest, wood breaking, a robed figure slumped unmoving in a throne of bones. Fire.

Mallory shook her head, groaning. She had slept through the day again. Outside the window, shreds of cloud raced across the sky, teasing the city below with glimpses of a crescent moon and an early scattering of stars.

At the sound of bone clattering on wood, Mallory turned her gaze from the window. From her dressing table twin lights of poison green glared at her. Shivering,

she struck a match and held it to the stub of candle beside her bed. Pulling damp blankets to her neck, she sat up.

The skull rattled away from her again. "Maggoty is not talking to anyone whose name is Mallsy-Ballsy-Hoopla-Boo-di-Bum-Bum," he announced.

"You're upset," Mallory said, her voice calm.

"La la la la la la la. Did you hear something, Maggoty? No, Maggoty, Maggoty did not. Must've been wind."

Mallory sighed. "You're going to be difficult, aren't you?"

The skull screeched. Jawbone clattering, he turned back to face Mallory. "*Difficult!* The *shade* of it all! Put poor Maggoty back in his box, eh?" he shrieked. "After all the wacky adventures Mallory and Maggoty have been through! All the zany stunts they've pulled together?"

"I found you less than two days ago," Mallory reminded the skull. "We've had exactly one wacky adventure."

"*Ouches*, Malls. Maggoty is deeply wounded by these vicious remarks. Pff, it's because Maggoty's a skull, isn't it? That's skullism, that is. The ugly face of anti-skullery. *Hurrumph!*"

"This is serious," Mallory said, glaring. "Do you think I want to raise the evil dead? You don't understand!"

"No, *you* don't understand," squealed the skull. "The important thing is Maggoty's feelings are hurt."

"What?" said Mallory, blinking. "You think that's the important thing?"

"Mallory said she'd take Maggoty's wig away, and shove him back in the box," the skull moaned. "She did, she did, she did."

"So help me, then," Mallory yelled. "Hellysh is offering me the chance to get my life back. I can go home, with my parents. My ma and da. *Alive.* We can be a family again. All this ... haunted castles and barmy aunts and séances and talking skulls and horrible, *horrible* necromancy ... it would be just a bad dream. Everything could go back to *normal.*"

Maggoty giggled. "Normal, she says," he crowed. "Maggoty doesn't think so, Boo."

"I have to try," Mallory protested.

"Silly, silly Mallory. That sort of necromancy will change you."

"I thought that was what you wanted," Mallory said through gritted teeth. "What happened to 'find yourself' and 'use your talents' and 'be who you're born to be' and blah, blah, blah."

"Yeah, well, there's discovering your inner necromancer and there's—"

"What you're forgetting is that I *had* found myself," Mallory shouted over him. "I was happy. Myself was just another boring girl and the talent I liked using was sitting quietly reading a book about ponies. Now look at me: arguing with a skull about raising the dead in a filthy, falling-down castle. Do you think I'm *enjoying* this?"

Tears rolled down Mallory's face. "I *hate* it," she sobbed. "I hate this castle. I hate necromancy. I hate Hellysh Spatzl. But I have no choice. I want my life back. I want my mother and father safe and home."

"Mallory," said the skull, his voice softer now. "We're getting off the point. The point is: what about Maggoty's feelings? Hmm? *Hello!*"

Wiping her eyes, Mallory sat up straighter and lifted her head. "Your feelings," she said, her voice cold. "Why should I care about *your* feelings? You don't care about *mine*. We're not friends, Maggoty. We have a deal. That's all."

The lights in Maggoty's eye sockets faded a little. "We're ... not ... friends?" he said slowly.

Mallory frowned at the skull. "Did you think we were? A friend would understand. Or at least try to understand.

A friend wouldn't think about themself all the time."

"Umm … Maggoty thinks you'll find you're wrong, Mallory Wrong. Maggoty's a cheeky but loveable rogue with a twinkle in his eye but—"

"Oh stop," Mallory scowled. "And stop pretending you care. You only care about Maggoty Skull. So, we're not friends. But help me and you can keep the wig and stay out of the box."

Green lights in Maggoty's eye sockets blinked hopefully. "And the curse?"

Mallory's eyes narrowed. "If … if you help me, I'll do what I can. That was the deal."

"The deal. Yes. The deal. The deal-a-roooni. The dealster. All righty-roo, Boo. So long as Maggoty's curse gets lifted then maybe it's no moss off Maggoty's skull if Mallory wants to raise the dead. What's the worst that could happen, eh?"

Mallory shrugged. Whatever the dangers, she had to save her mother and father. "So you'll help?" she asked.

"So long as Maggoty's curse gets broken."

Mallory drummed her fingers against her cheek. "Do you have any idea how I do that?" she asked.

"Nopetty nope. Zero. Zilch. Strangely, Hellysh did not

give poor Maggoty a user's guide. All she did was cackle and say there was a way but Maggoty would never ever ever find anyone willing to pay the price."

"The *price*?" Mallory gulped. "There's a price now?"

"Well, *duh*," Maggoty chortled. "It's a curse. There's *always* a price. If you're lucky, Boo, it'll be one of them true-love's-kiss-based curses. Sweet, cherry lips and all that. Hmm. Are you – Mallory Ballory Buttcrack – truly, madly, deeply in love with Maggoty yet?"

"Umm … no," said Mallory, shaking her head. "Not even a little bit."

"Give it a day or two," said Maggoty, sounding confident. "It'll happen. Anyhoo, whatever sort of curse it is, it'll be in Hellysh's diary, so up and at 'em. Despicable, soul-twisting rituals to perform. Corpses to raise. *A-rang-dang-digetty-dang-a-dang.*"

Mallory filed Maggoty's curse under 'Things to Worry About Later'. "I suppose that means starting with Aunt Lilith," she said. "She might remember who she sold the diary to."

Maggoty's jaw rattled on the dressing table. "All right, let's do this thang. Oooh, and look: it's almost night time again. Perfect for dubious deeds and dark goings-on.

Look at you, Boo. Waking up at the crack of dusk, eh? Rising with the moon. Classic creature of the night."

Creature of the night.

A shiver ran down Mallory's spine as she clambered out of bed and dressed. She was turning into something from a horror story. Worse, she had to go and talk to her aunt. She had been dreading it since Mrs Hadley's séance.

She found her aunt sitting at the kitchen table, sucking the end of a pencil and hunched over a sheet of paper, surrounded by dribbling candles, packs of cards, a crystal ball, several cups containing tea leaves, and bowls of smoking herbs. Today's dress spread around her in wafts of black lace. A wide-brimmed black hat and heavy veil made her look like a depressed bee-keeper. For a few moments, Mallory hung back and watched from the doorway while her aunt mumbled, shuffling cards and laying them out before scribbling on her sheet of paper. "Three of Pillocks and the Dread Lord of Agony in the events-yet-to-come position," she murmured. "*Interesting.* The Three of Pillocks means foolishness in love, and the Dread Lord of Agony speaks to us of cooked

meat. Will someone propose marriage to a slice of ham next Thursday? Who? Speak, Mr Lozenge. What's that? I'm getting the name Sponge… Graham Sponge, is it, Mr Lozenge?"

While she jotted the name down, Mallory cleared her throat.

Aunt Lilith looked up. "Oh, Mallory. There you are. I thought you were going to sleep for ever." Pausing, she glanced at the skull Mallory was carrying and blinked. "Umm … err … oh … I wondered why you needed a wig so urgently but I didn't guess it would be for the skull.

Why is your skull wearing that revolting wig, darling?"

"*Revolting*! How utterly dare she!" the skull's voice squealed in Mallory's ear. "Maggoty demands we torture her."

"He likes it," said Mallory, setting Maggoty on the table.

Her aunt waited for Mallory to say more. When that didn't happen she mumbled, "Yes, yes. Of course he does. Silly of me. Oh, I made some porridge. Would you like some?"

Mallory's stomach rumbled. "Yes, please," she said. Taking a seat, she watched silently, as her aunt crossed to the stove, pushing aside cobwebs in the gloom. The train of her dress swept the floor as she walked, which Mallory thought was probably a new experience for the floor. "Uh … we haven't really spoken since … since Mrs Hadley," she continued, blushing and trying not to hear Maggoty's furious ranting. "I'm sorry I called you a fraud. I'm … ahh… It had been a difficult night and it was rude…"

"Sweetheart," her aunt cried, clapping her hands together. Bangles and bracelets jangled. "I admit I was shocked at first, but it was simply *marvellous. You* were

marvellous. I have never seen such a *shattering* display of psychic talent."

"But I said…"

"Tish and piff."

"And I … I…"

"Hush now, there's a good girl. No. No, Mallory, shush. We didn't get off to the best start, perhaps, but that's all over now, *hmm*? Look at you, carrying skulls around. You're simply *bursting*, like a darling, darling sausage sizzling with delicious psychic talent." Aunt Lilith clapped again. "What messages are you picking up from the beyond today, precious? Chatter of spotlights, I expect. Sold-out theatre tours, books… You'll be famous. A star! Oh, it's all so exciting, and – of course – dear Aunt Lilith will be there to guide you as you show off your exceptional spiritual gifts to the world."

Mallory blinked at her aunt: "What?"

"People have been simply *banging* away at the door. They all want appointments with you, and I've had a wonderful idea. We'll make an absolute fortune."

Mallory gasped "Appointments? What appointments?"

"For psychic readings, you goose. Mrs Hadley went straight home and found a bank book in the shed, just where you said it would be! Five *hundred* pounds. She told her friends, and her friends told *their* friends. Now everyone wants to see you."

Mallory glanced down. Her spine froze. Among her aunt's cards and cups and made-up messages from the dead was a note that Aunt Lilith had doodled on and underlined.

Grand Séance, with star attraction – the incredible, soon-to-be World-Famous MALLORY VAYLE. Experience the WONDER of the world's most gifted psychic for only FIVE SHILLINGS!

CHAPTER 14

Mallory gasped, looking up to glare at her aunt. "Grand Séance?" she said, her voice going high.

"It's a *marvellous* idea, don't you think?" Aunt Lilith chuckled as she crossed the kitchen carrying a bowl. "What better way to show off your talents? And think of the money, darling!"

"The *money*?" said Mallory, her glare turning into a scowl.

"And the spiritual comfort we could bring to our audience. Yes, yes: spiritual comfort. It's *sooo* important, isn't it? Bringing joy into the drab, miserable lives of everyday folk. The money would be useful, though. We could get the old place done up, you know, and—"

Mallory blinked. "I'm not doing any more psychic readings. And I'm *definitely* not being displayed like a circus freak in front of an audience."

"Darling." Aunt Lilith stopped in the middle of the kitchen, then continued: "Darling, darling, darling." Adding another "darling" she seemed to realise that she might have gone a bit overboard with the word. To change things up, she said, "Sweetheart," instead.

"NO," Mallory insisted.

"But you have a gift, Mallory."

"I said, *no.*"

Aunt Lilith dropped a bowl containing what appeared to be a chunk of porridge in front of her niece before sagging into the chair opposite. The smile fell from her face. "That's a shame," she said. "Because Mrs Hadley was my only customer and no one will want a psychic reading with *me* now. You'd better eat your porridge while we still have food in the house."

Mallory blinked at her. "You're poor? But you live in a castle!"

Her aunt paused, took a sip of foul-smelling herbal tea and leaned back in her chair. "The castle is all I have. I *was* poor, dear. Now I'm penniless."

Mallory poked at her porridge brick. It made a faint clunking sound. Returning her attention to her aunt, she said quietly, "I'm sorry, Aunt Lilith. I'm sorry I called you a fraud and I'm sorry I lost your only customer, but... No, never mind." She stopped, reminding herself that she needed information from her aunt. An argument wouldn't help her get it, and if everything went to plan she would soon be leaving Carrion Castle, psychic readings and grand séances far, far behind. "Aunt Lilith," she continued, trying to keep irritation out of her voice. "We can talk about that later. Right now, I wanted to ask you a question."

"A question? Of course. Ask Aunty Lilith anything. Is it about the lavatory? You have to pull the chain, wait fifteen seconds, then pull it again. It will work then."

"No, but thank you," said Mallory. "I have been wondering about that. I wanted to ask about a book, though."

"A book?" said her aunt, as if she vaguely remembered what books were.

"Yes. You know: words, paper, flippy pages. Sometimes pictures. There was a book here. At Carrion Castle. A very old book. The diary of someone called Hellysh Spatzl.

The … ahh … spirits … yes, the spirits … told me you sold it."

"*Hmm* … that's possible. I've sold a lot of things that were lying around the old place. Business has been slow, and candles are so expensive nowadays. Your skull really does look ridiculous in that wig, Mallory. I'm not against you carrying a skull around, darling. It's quite charming and simply *screams* 'psychic', but is the wig really, truly necessary, do you think?"

"Is a punch in the throat really, truly necessary?" the skull muttered.

"Getting back to the book," Mallory went on soothingly, while Maggoty listed all the ways he would like to torture Aunt Lilith. "Who did you sell it to?"

Aunt Lilith shuffled cards, looking thoughtful. "There were lots of old books here," she said with a shrug. "Written in languages. *Languages!* As if that wasn't bad enough, some of them were full of beastly drawings. Goats, dear. That's all I'm saying. Quite, *quite* disturbing. I will never understand…" Her aunt's voice trailed off. Suddenly trembling, she stared at the wall over Mallory's shoulder. "What … what was that?"

Mallory glanced over her shoulder and saw only her

shadow, cast against a grimy wall by the candlelight. "What was what?" she asked.

"Your shadow," hissed her aunt. "It was *looking* at me."

"Heh," Maggoty chuckled. "You're doing shadow play without even thinking about it. Maggoty told you, Boo. *Rama-lama-lama-dinky-da-dinky-donk.* You're becoming a – mwah-ha-HA – creature of the night."

Mallory paled, glaring at her own shadow, which sat, mirroring her movements, its hair in a neat bun. "It must have been the candle flickering," she said, turning back to her aunt. "I need that book, Aunt Lilith."

"I swear it moved," breathed her aunt, staring at the wall. "It threw its hands up. It was … it was *annoyed* with me."

A chill trickled down Mallory's spine. Annoyed was exactly how she felt. Taking a breath, she said, "Shadows can't move. Well, they can but not … well, you know what I mean. Aunt Lilith, can we *please* talk about the book?"

"What book?"

"The book I've been telling you about for the last five minutes," Mallory said, her voice betraying just a touch of irritation. "Ancient diary. Remember?"

"I suppose it *must* have been a trick of the light," Aunt Lilith murmured. Snapping her attention back to Mallory, she continued. "Why on *Earth* would you want some silly old book with pictures of nasty goats?"

Mallory bit her lip. "The ... err ... the spirits said it was important," she said.

"I see," said her aunt, looking unconvinced. "How's your porridge? I've heard it's full of healthy something or other. Growing young bodies, hmm?"

Mallory took a deep breath and crunched a spoonful of porridge with her back teeth. Trying to keep her voice light and pleasant, she said, "Please try and remember, Aunt Lilith."

Her aunt flapped a hand. "My sweet angel, forget about books. You'll never find anything interesting in books. What truly matters is in your *heart*."

"That's the most stupid thing I've ever heard..." Mallory started. "Sorry, I mean I really need that book."

"That's a shame because I haven't the foggiest idea what I did with it."

"Are you sure?" Screwing her face up, Mallory forced the next sentence out through her teeth. "If you helped me find it then perhaps, maybe, we could talk about your

Grand Séance."

Aunt Lilith gasped, clasping her hands over her heart. *"Really?"* she gasped, breathless. "That would be just ... just *divine*, you sweet, *sweet* lamb. We'll have to get you a new dress, of course. And do something with your hair and—"

"Book first," Mallory reminded her.

"But I'm afraid I really don't remember it, or who I might have sold it to. I'm *quite* the scatterbrain, you know."

Mallory groaned. If the book was lost then so too were her chances of getting her life back.

"But if it's so important to you, dear, maybe the cards will help," Aunt Lilith went on, reaching for a deck and beginning to shuffle.

"Oh, great, the cards." Mallory sighed under her breath. Along with everything else Aunt Lilith had forgotten, it seemed to have slipped her mind that she had no psychic talent whatsoever.

A card flipped on to the table. Mallory dropped her gaze to see a picture of a wizened gnome leering up at her. "The Nonger," her aunt said. "Thank you, Mr Lozenge. We seek a short, big-nosed, bad-tempered stranger. Hmm."

She shuffled again. "Can you clarify that, Mr Lozenge?"

Gently, Mallory took the cards from her aunt's hands. "I don't think Mr Lozenge is at home, Aunt Lilith," she murmured. "Why don't you try to *remember* instead?"

Without thinking, Mallory began toying with the cards while staring into her aunt's face, cutting the pack and – *frrrrp* – riffling the two halves back together again. Behind her, unseen, her shadow drummed soundlessly on the shadow table with dark fingers.

"Well, I'll try, but..." her aunt began, misty-eyed behind her veil as she studied her black painted fingernails. "Hmmm ... no ... no. I'm sorry, Mallory, but I simply cannot recall what might have happened to one book. I sold lots of things. That's why Carrion Castle is so empty."

Frustrated, Mallory's grip tightened around the cards she was holding.

She squeezed too hard. With a sound like a startled flock of birds taking off, the entire deck burst from her hand and flew into the air.

"Oh!" Leaning back in her chair, Mallory watched while cards showered to the floor in a flurry of colourful twirling images. Cats and sunflowers, grinning beasts and shameless nudists fell past Mallory's eyes.

"Oh," she repeated as she watched them fall into a pattern.

Behind her, Mallory's shadow leaned forward.

"Oh," Aunt Lilith echoed, as the last card fluttered to rest. It became the dot under an exclamation point.

Spread across the floor the cards spelled out, in perfect capital letters, HARRY GIZZARD'S HOUSE OF CURIOSITIES!

CHAPTER 15

Cold wind hunted dead leaves down the cobbled alleys of Stabbings, hustling its prey into doorways where they panicked, whirling in dizzying circles. A few pressed themselves up against windows as if pleading to be let in, before tumbling and fluttering away into darkness, chased by the chilly blast.

Mallory and her aunt walked the dingy, narrow streets with the fleeing leaves, their skirts and Aunt Lilith's veil whipping. The skull beneath Mallory's arm squealed whenever the gale threatened to snatch his wig off.

"You didn't need to come, Aunt Lilith," Mallory shouted over the wind.

"Oh, darling, I'm caught up in the drama," her aunt

replied, one hand keeping her hat in place. "When the cards fell like that I almost died, Mallory. Honestly. I've never seen such a powerful message from the spirits. What can it mean? What is this oh-so-mysterious book? It's all so exciting. Besides, you don't know these streets and… Oh, here we are. This is the place."

The dark shop front was hardly more than a doorway wide, its tiny window dimly lit from within and stuffed with faded items, including one clown shoe and a live tortoise. Over the door, the wind bullied an old and flaking sign into swinging wildly, making it shriek in a rusty voice.

Harry Gizzard's House of Curiosities.

"The memories are *flooding* back now, Mallory," Aunt Lilith twittered. "About five years ago I sold Mr Gizzard a pile of junk, including a book. I remember because he was a very strange little man."

Wondering just how strange someone would have to be for Aunt Lilith to think they were odd, Mallory pushed the door open. Leaves squeezed past into safety and lay gasping on the floor as she and her aunt stepped inside. "Umm ... hello?" Mallory called, gazing around.

The tiny shop was lit by a cracked lamp that cast a jigsaw of shadows over a space crammed so tight there was barely room for Mallory and her aunt to stand. Broken dolls peered at them through blank eyes, a harp with snapped strings stuck out from boxes of junk like the prow of a ship had crashed through the wall. In one corner a full human skeleton hung from a hook.

"Friend of yours?" Mallory whispered, giving Maggoty a jiggle.

Maggoty sniffed. "Would you look at her, just dangling there. Make an effort, dear."

"*Hello*, Mr Gizzard," said Aunt Lilith loudly, tinkling a bell she found half-hidden on the counter.

From the back of the shop came a rustling sound.

Through a doorway, Mallory saw a small figure stir from its seat in the centre of a cramped sitting room, not far from a spindly fire. Wearing a scowl, a nightshirt and a long, tasselled night cap, white hair straying from beneath, a gnome-like man made mostly of nose elbowed his way through clutter and shuffled to the counter, where he climbed on to a box and leered at his customers.

Turning to her niece, Aunt Lilith whispered, "The Nonger, you see. What did the cards tell us about a short, big-nosed, bad-tempered person?"

Mallory found herself nodding. Just this once, her aunt's cards were quite accurate. Mr Gizzard did look very much like The Nonger.

"Eh?" croaked the shopkeeper, shooting both Mallory and her aunt an ugly squint each. "Who are you? What do you want? Coming in here bold as celery and dragging an old man off the toilet."

"I was just telling my niece that my spirit guide – Mr Lozenge – has shown us the path to your shop," said Aunt Lilith. "Now, if you please, we've come about—"

"I'll give you tuppence for it," wheezed Mr Gizzard.

"Two pence? For what?" Mallory answered.

"For the skull. Wig included. Don't try and swindle me

out of the wig."

"It's ... err ... not for sale," Mallory told him.

"What do you want, then? Oooh, I know *your* tricks. Come to rob a poor old man, eh? That's how you young folk get your fun, isn't it? Hit me with a knobbly stick 'til I'm half-dead then run off laughing with my life's savings."

"I don't have a knobbly stick, Mr Gizzard," Mallory said calmly. "I just wanted to—"

"Knobbly stick, three shillings," said Mr Gizzard, reaching below the counter and laying a knobbly stick on top of the teetering pile of junk on the counter.

This, Mallory thought, answered her question. Someone would have to be very strange indeed to be considered a weirdo by Aunt Lilith. "I don't want a knobbly stick," she replied.

"How about big boots, then?" snapped the old man, adding a pair of boots about ten sizes too large for Mallory to the pile on the counter. "Four shillings. Wrestle me to the floor and with these boots – hardly worn, look at the quality – you could kick me to a pulp in just a few moments. I'll throw in the knobbly stick for a shilling."

Mallory blinked at the old man. "What?"

"Mr Gizzard," Aunt Lilith interrupted. "No one is here to kick anyone to a pulp. Please try to stop being so very, very unhinged."

The little man jabbed a finger at her. "I know *your* type. Oh, yes, I see your game. Pulling an old man's underwear up over his head then chasing the poor chap around the streets for everyone to have a good old laugh at, isn't it?" Laying a set of old man's stained underwear on the counter, the little man fixed Aunt Lilith with a glare, coughed, and said. "A shilling and sixpence."

"Mr GIZZARD," Aunt Lilith insisted, rapping on a small, uncluttered space on the counter. "We came to ask about a book."

"Maggoty wants that suit," the skull chipped in. "The one with black and white stripes. *Gorgeous*. Maggoty will look st – un – ning in it."

Without thinking, Mallory turned her head, spotting the suit Maggoty was talking about on the rack. "Don't you think it's a bit ... umm ... loud?" she whispered before stopping herself. "You can't have a suit," she finished.

"Why not? Maggoty wants a suit. Want, want, want, want, want."

"You haven't got a body, you idiot," Mallory hissed under her breath, turning her attention back to her aunt and Mr Gizzard's conversation.

"You must remember! I sold it to you only a few years ago," Aunt Lilith was saying.

"Ain't got no books," replied Mr Gizzard, sounding sulky. "No call for 'em. Don't stock books, see? Tell you what, though. Gimme the skull and the wig for half a shilling and I'll throw in a free book." Reaching below the counter, he added a book to the pile. "*Debbie Turns into a Potato*," he announced.

"We don't want *Debbie Turns into a Potato*," Mallory explained, trying to make her voice sound patient. "We're looking for an old diary. It's—"

"Quickly, please, Mr Gizzard. We don't have all night," said Aunt Lilith, rapping the counter again.

"If you still have it, we'd like to buy it back. At a slightly higher price than you paid, of course," Mallory finished.

"Higher price, eh?" Mr Gizzard peered at Mallory, who nodded.

"I'll give you *Debbie Turns into a Potato* for five pounds."

"You just offered it to us free!"

"Four pounds, then. And I'll throw in the knobbly stick."

Through clenched teeth, Mallory said, "We don't want *Debbie Turns into a Potato*. We don't want a knobbly stick, and we don't want to beat you up. At least, we didn't when we came in. If you still have it we will offer a fair price for the book we want, which – to be completely clear – is an ancient diary NOT *Debbie Turns into a Potato*." Seeing Mr Gizzard open his mouth, she held up a finger. "If you don't have it we can offer a small reward if you can tell us who you sold it to."

Harry Gizzard peered at her, eyes glinting. "You want a book?" he said. "A book what this lady sold me about five years ago? That book?"

"Yes," said Mallory with a sigh of relief. "That book."

"And you don't want to knee me in the unmentionables and run away laughing?"

Mallory shook her head.

"You really, *really* want that book, eh?"

"Yes, Mr Gizzard. We really, really want that book."

"Wait here." Mr Gizzard jumped off his box and disappeared into the back room. For a few minutes,

Mallory and her aunt heard loud crashes and bangs and a mechanical voice saying, "Ooh, I done another one, Kitty." Eventually, Mr Gizzard returned with a large, blood-red leather book clutched in his bony hands.

"This it?" he sniffed, dropping it to the counter with a dusty thump.

Reaching out, Mallory lifted the cover and ran her fingers across pages crammed with faded ink. The writing was broken with strange diagrams, step-by-step drawings, and pictures of goats. The pages thrummed with necromancy. Under Mallory's hands the diary of Hellysh Spatzl felt almost alive.

She nodded, whispering, "Yes. This is it."

"As I recall, I sold it to you for three shillings," said Aunt Lilith, digging into a clinking purse. "So, I suggest we double that and give you six generous, shiny shillings. Does that sound like a splendid deal, Mr Gizzard?"

Mr Gizzard scowled. Closing the book with a snap that made Mallory snatch her fingers back, he sniffed again, and said, "No. It don't. I couldn't let such a vallyble antique go for a penny less than a hundred pounds."

"How much?" gasped Mallory and her aunt at the same time.

"You heard me," Mr Gizzard said. "Seeing as how you really, *really* want this book, the price is one hundred pounds."

CHAPTER 16

Ignoring sad-faced ghosts that stared down from cracked windows as well as alive-but-shabby Stabbings residents shuffling past, Mallory groaned. "A *hundred* pounds," she growled as she and her aunt made their way back through dark alleys. "A hundred pounds! That horrid, cheating little goblin. Where am I going to find a hundred pounds?"

"Get back there, Mallsy," Maggoty squawked. "Squirl the old tonker's brain with your wicked arts. Once he's eating his own hair, pinch the book. Pull his underwear up over his head too. That'll add a nice touch. Ooh, and beat him with the knobbly stick. Maggoty hates seeing a perfectly good knobbly stick go to waste."

"Shush," Mallory hissed, turning into a narrow alley.

Aunt Lilith squealed. "Your shadow, Mallory! It's doing it again."

Mallory spun on the spot. Her shadow stretched out long on the cobbles, cast by the light of a fizzing gas lamp. Dark fists were clenching and unclenching.

Mallory swore quietly. Her shadow looked like she felt: *angry*. "I … I…" She took a deep breath. Rippling, the shadow returned to normal, but it was too late. This time there would be no explaining its curious behaviour as a trick of the light.

Aunt Lilith was still staring wide-eyed at the cobbles. "Darling," she said, her voice sounding faraway. "Call me a silly muffin but I'm starting to think that you're not just a simple psychic."

Mallory squeezed her eyes closed. Opening them, she shook her head. "No," she said. "No. I'm not."

"What *are* you?" Aunt Lilith's voice sounded scared, but unexpectedly gentle. Mallory looked up to see she had pushed back her veil. It blew in the wind.

Their eyes met.

"I'm *miserable*," Mallory croaked. "My parents are dead. They've been taken by a horrible spirit and ... and ... I think I might be evil. But I don't want to be evil. I just want to be normal."

"Oh, my sweet, sweet girl," said Aunt Lilith, taking Mallory's chin and giving it an affectionate pinch. "No one is *normal*. At least, no one interesting. Haven't you learned that yet? Normal is for people too scared to be themselves, don't you think? And it's so very, very dull."

"I'd rather be dull than ... than ... this," Mallory whispered, blinking back tears.

"Sheesh," said Maggoty. "Boo hoo. Maggoty hates to interrupt this pathetic sob-fest, but look behind—"

"Oh, shut up," Mallory snapped. Seeing her aunt flinch, she added quickly, "Not you, Aunt Lilith. The skull. Maggoty. He's an insensitive clod."

"The skull?" Aunt Lilith glanced down at Maggoty. "It really *does* speak to you? You don't just carry it around to look spooky?"

"Insensitive clod?" interrupted Maggoty, outraged. "Clod? *Hmmph*. We'll come back to that later. For right now, you should—"

"Yes, he really does speak to me," Mallory sniffed, ignoring him. "Though I wish he wouldn't, most of the time. Wigs, wigs, wigs. That's all he talks about."

"Again: *ouches*. But if you want to get mugged it's none of Maggoty's business."

"Mugged?" snapped Mallory. "What nonsense are you spouting now?"

A figure stepped out of the darkness behind Aunt Lilith. A large figure. A large figure wearing a filthy, patched brown suit with no shirt underneath – just a stained scarf tied around its neck. A dented bowler hat was perched on its meaty head.

The figure dropped a hand on Aunt Lilith's lacy shoulder and gripped tight, making her squeal again. "Evenin', ladies," it said in a low voice. "My name is Snaggles – not my real name – and I will be yer mugger this evening."

"Second thoughts – let's talk about the clod thing now," sniffed the skull. "*Rude*, Mallsy."

"Maggoty," whispered Mallory.

"What ... what do I do?"

"Wigs," the skull snapped back. "That's all Maggoty talks about. Wigs, wigs, wigs."

"Nice skull," Snaggles grinned. "Reminds me of someone I *murdered* last week. Now, keeping nice and quiet, hand over any money or jewellery you might have about your persons, eh?"

"We don't have any money," Mallory told him.

"Touch my niece, you brute, and I shall rain down curses upon you," said Aunt Lilith, struggling. "I can, you know. I'm a trained—"

The mugger's fingers gripped Aunt Lilith's shoulders tighter. "Brute!" she whimpered again. "Let us go. We're psychics."

"Psychics, eh? Did yer see this coming?" Snaggles pulled a knife from his belt. The edge glimmered with reflected moonlight as he twisted it before Aunt Lilith's eyes.

She screamed quietly.

"I'll take that as a 'no'," Snaggles chuckled. "And that brings us to the end of the playful chit-chat portion of yer mugging. On to the part where I take yer stuff. It is strongly recommended you hands it over without a fuss, thusly avoiding unpleasantness."

"No," said Mallory, standing taller. Confusion vanished. Dark necromancy boiled in her stomach and tingled down her arms.

Behind her – unnoticed by the mugger – her shadow's hair dropped out of its bun, once more curling to dark shoulders. It stretched, cricking its neck as if preparing for a fight.

"*No?*" growled Snaggles, raising the knife to Aunt Lilith's throat. "I'm afraid you've mistaken old Snaggles fer someone who takes 'no' for an answer."

"Mallory, dear," squeaked Aunt Lilith. "I think, perhaps…"

"I said, *no*," Mallory snarled, lifting Maggoty.

Without understanding what she was doing or how she was doing it, necromancy flowed from Mallory's stomach, down her arms and through her fingertips in tiny purple sparks. Maggoty's eyes flared brighter. Aunt Lilith yelped as the narrow alley turned green.

"Wha—" Snaggles choked. His gaze flicked to the wall behind Mallory. "Maah," he squeaked. Her shadow was growing. Hair flowed loose around its shoulders, its hands lengthened into claws…

"*Yaaas*, Malls. This is more like it," cheered the skull. "Look, he's *wetting* himself! He's actually weeing down his own leg, right now! See, there's a little puddle round his feet. Eww. Gross but also hi-*laaaar*-i-ous. Now that's what Maggoty calls quality entertainment."

Snaggles' gaze dropped back to the skull in Mallory's hand. With a clang, the knife dropped from his hand on to the wet cobbles. "Gah," the mugger croaked.

Aunt Lilith gasped, staring at the skull. "It's … it's … *alive*…" she croaked.

"Oooh, they can hear me too," gasped the skull. "*Yeee-hah*. Maggoty Skull's got messages from the beyond for you, Mr Wee-Wee Pants Snaggles," he croaked in a spooky voice. "Are you ready?"

Making choking noises, Snaggles took
a step backwards, his boots sloshing.

"First," crooned Maggoty, "what's with that
suit? Brown? No. Just no. What were you thinking? And
the patches. What are we trying to say here? If you're
going to do patches make them a feature. Second—"

"*Maggoty*," hissed Mallory.

"Oh, right," said the skull. His voice
dropped into a low groan. "Let's
start again. Maggoty's message
is GO. Run away before Maggs
and Mallsy get nasty. Go on. GO. Get. LOST."

As the skull's voice growled in the mugger's ears,
Mallory squeezed her eyes closed. With a thought, her
shadow burst behind her, breaking into a thousand dark
bats that exploded across walls and the
cobbles below.

"Aaaaaargghhhh!" Snaggles screamed. "Nooooo. Leave me alone. Don't. Aaaarghh—"

"GO!" shrieked the skull.

Still screaming, Snaggles turned and ran, chased by bat-shaped shadows. Damp trousers flapped around his ankles.

"Bwah ha ha ha HA HA HA," cackled Maggoty. "Did you hear Maggoty? Wee-Wee Pants, he called him! Brilliant, eh? Oh, Maggoty, you *do* make Maggoty laugh. Ha ha ha ha HA HA HA!"

While the skull babbled, Mallory and her aunt stared at each other as Snaggles' screams and the sound of his running feet faded into the distance. With a sigh, Mallory put her hand to her head where a few strands of her hair had come loose from her bun. Wind whipped them around her face. Lights went out in the skull's eye sockets. Maggoty's laughter faded. Shadow bats returned, pouring into one another, forming the shadow of a girl holding a skull that was wearing a wig.

"Wh-what are you, Mallory?" Aunt Lilith gurgled eventually.

Turning to her wide-eyed, trembling aunt, Mallory said quietly, "I'm a necromancer."

"A... A... *what*?"

Her niece sighed. "Let's go home and put the kettle on, shall we, Aunt Lilith?" she said. "I'll explain everything. Then we can talk about how we can make a hundred pounds."

CHAPTER 17

A lonely bell chimed midnight somewhere across the city rooftops. The distant sound broke the silence in the kitchen of Carrion Castle. Mallory rapped her knuckles on the kitchen table. "Aunt Lilith," she said. "Aunt *Lilith*."

Her aunt didn't look up. Her eyes stayed fixed on Maggoty Skull. "It *speaks*," she croaked. "I *heard* it. The skull speaks."

"Can we torture her?" sighed Maggoty. "Just a little bit."

"No. Shush. Sorry, Aunt Lilith. Yes, the skull speaks. We've been through this sixteen times. There's a spirit trapped inside and he yammers on way past the point of annoying." Mallory ignored the farting noise Maggoty made in response.

Aunt Lilith gulped. Her eyes nervously flicked to Mallory's. "And you can hear it ... because ... because you're a *necromancer*." Her aunt pronounced the word as if she had a mouthful of slugs.

Mallory nodded, feeling a blush of shame colour her face. "If it helps, I suppose you could just think of me as a *really* good psychic."

"Necromancy," whispered her aunt, shivering. "I've heard stories. It's ... it's pointy beards and names like Mouldwart, isn't it? Are you – how can I put this? – are you a dark and midnight hag, Mallory?"

"Huh," Maggoty chipped in. "Dark and midnight hag! Party. That'd be *waaaay* too much fun for Mallsy."

Mallory glared at him. "No," she said, answering her aunt's question. "At least, I hope not. Not yet, at least. Once I've found my parents' ghosts, I hope I can ... well, give it up."

"Ha ha ha ha ha ha ha HA HA HA. Did Maggoty mention HA HA HA? Give it up. Oh, that's a good one."

Mallory paused, feeling guilty that she'd told her aunt only part of the truth. After two hours and six cups of tea, her aunt was still struggling with the news that her niece was a necromancer. Mallory was fairly

certain telling her about dark rituals that would bring an ancient necromancer – and her own parents – back from the grave would tip her over the edge. "Can we change the subject now?" she said. "A very bad ghost has my parents trapped and the only way to get them back is in that book. We need to make money. Fast."

"But ... but necromancy, dear," her aunt murmured. "Ugh. Lurking in tombs. Grave robbing. Stitching together body parts to make lurching, patchwork monsters that terrorise the local community. As your legal guardian, I'm afraid I must draw the line at terrorising the local community. It gives entirely the wrong impression of modern psychics. Stitching body parts together is also a no-no."

"But I've been practising my needlework."

"Mallory!"

"I'm joking, Aunt Lilith," said Mallory, hoping that was true. For all she knew the ritual to bring back Hellysh Spatzl might indeed mean stitching together body parts. "Money, remember? Can we talk about the money now?"

"I mean, obviously I want to be supportive. *Obviously*. But it's a lot to take in." Aunt Lilith nibbled a fingernail. "You're sure your parents' spirits haven't just gone into

the light? Ghosts do that, you know. They might have fallen in by accident. Lumpy always was quite clumsy."

"Could you please not call my ma Lumpy?" Mallory paused. "Forget it. Look, believe me, Aunt Lilith, an evil spirit has taken them and won't release them until I get that book."

"But *why* do you need this book?" Aunt Lilith insisted. "What does this horrid spirit want?"

Mallory bit her lip. "I don't know," she lied. "Please, Aunt Lilith. I need to buy that book. I'll do as many psychic readings as it takes, and your Grand Séance too." With a big-eyed look, she added, *"Please."*

At last Aunt Lilith's face brightened slightly. "It would be a chance for us to get to know each other better, wouldn't it?"

Mallory nodded eagerly. "And I'll wear whatever you like and do my hair however you want," she promised. "You've seen what I can do. We'll put on an amazing show."

"Now this is a Mallory who Maggoty could grow to love," warbled the skull. "Give 'em the old razzle dazzle, eh? Da-da-di-dum-*BOO*! Lights! Curtains! Tap dancing, leotards and sparkly hats! Skin-shrivelling horror. Yay!"

Thanking her lucky stars her aunt could no longer hear the skull, Mallory watched Aunt Lilith's thoughts chase across her pale, painted face. Mallory could almost see her imagination conjuring piles of cash. "Weeell," Aunt Lilith said slowly. "I suppose if you're careful, and if it means freeing your parents' spirits from the clutches of some beastly phantom…"

"Great," said Mallory. "Where do we begin?"

Aunt Lilith thought about it. "Luckily, Daisy Hadley can't keep her mouth shut," she said. "She told anyone who'd listen about the money you found for her, and she's been swanking around all over the city showing off her new teeth. I've had people banging on door every five minutes. A few notices should be all we need."

Mallory nodded eagerly, reaching for a pen and a sheet of paper.

GRAND SÉANCE

This Halloween, why not discover the Secrets of the Supernatural at Carrion Castle? Hear voices from the beyond with your own *EARS*! See real, live *GHOSTS*, summoned for your *AMAZEMENT!*

Announcing a Grand Séance, with star attraction — the incredible psychic talents of

MALLORY VAYLE!

PLUS...

Card readings by Mistress of the Night, the one and only
LILITH NIGHTSHADE!

Tea and cake!

Tickets on sale *NOW*, priced five shillings.
Book early to avoid disappointment!

CHAPTER 18

Mallory had hardly finished pinning the first notice to a lamppost before people began knocking at the door of Carrion Castle. The rumours Daisy Hadley had already started were spreading at the lightning speed of gossip. In whispers, people told each other that Mallory Vayle was a really, *really* good psychic. She had made Daisy Hadley rich. None of the city's other psychics had ever made anyone rich. The only money they'd ever made had been for themselves.

Before lunchtime there was a queue of people waiting for tickets to the Grand Séance. By the time Mallory returned to her own room it was midnight once more. Still the thunderous door knocker boomed through

the castle every few minutes. Tickets were sold out and people were offering double – triple – the entrance fee. Mallory left her aunt wondering how many more seats they could cram into the grand hall while counting an enormous heap of coins. Lying back on her lumpy bed, she stared up at the cracked and stained ceiling. The night felt alive. Without looking over at the dressing table, she whispered, "Maggoty? Are you awake?"

"Well, *duh*," said the skull.

"Teach me something," Mallory said.

The skull stayed silent for a few moments, then said, "You're really going through with this, aren't you, Boo? You're going to raise Hellysh Spatzl."

"Yes," Mallory breathed. "And … and … I'm not in the slightest bit ready to perform necromancy like that." She paused, trying to find words. "About Hellysh…" she started. The temperature in the room dropped a couple of degrees. A rotting stench curled into Mallory's nose.

She shivered, looking around and seeing nothing but shadow.

"The *booook*," Hellysh's worms-in-a-coffin voice croaked from deep shadow. Shadow writhed on the wall behind Mallory. "Where isss it?"

"We're working on it," Mallory said, her voice shaking. "Give us a few days."

"The book. *NOW!*"

"It's going to cost a lot of money to buy it back," Mallory said. "Be patient."

"Noooooo patiencccce. *Book.*" Hellysh Spatzl sounded harsh.

"I'm doing my best," Mallory snapped, suddenly more angry than afraid. This time, a little necromancy leaked into her voice.

Let us … leave me alone … patience…

Words she had not used echoed softly from the walls.

Behind her, the shadow vanished. The temperature in Mallory's room rose until she could no longer see her breath frosting.

Maggoty's eyes twinkled. "*Brrr …* what a manky old grave dodger. Hey, you're getting better at using The Voice, Boo. Now, what was it you were saying before we were so rudely interrupted?"

"Nothing," Mallory said, hugging herself. "So, what else can you teach me?"

"Teach you, hmm? Maggoty could teach you something, yes. But Maggoty wouldn't want to yammer

on way past the point of being annoying."

"Just this once, maybe you could give the drama a rest." Mallory rolled her eyes, the memory of Hellysh already fading. The skull's nonsense, she admitted to herself, was strangely comforting.

"*Drama?*" the skull squealed. "Shudder! *Gasp!* How utterly *dare* you! HUFF! Maggoty's not talking to Mallory. *Again.*"

"Maggoty!" Before the skull could reply, she went on. "Could you just stop? I mean, we could argue the next hour or you could just get over yourself and teach me something useful."

"Oh, all right, then, you don't have to look at Maggoty like that. *Sigh.* Let's open *The Maggoty Guide to Necromancy.* So, we've completed the lesson on shadow play. You've learned how to give the ghosties some of your own power, and your necromancer's Voice is growing stronger. Let's turn to chapter four. What's this? Shadow walking. This Maggoty Skull-approved lesson will allow you to detach your own shadow and slip through the darkness. Guaranteed success. Or your money back. Wanna try?"

Mallory sat up and struck a match, lighting the candle

by her rickety bed. "Shadow walking," she said. "Hmm. Sounds interesting. Yes. Let's start there."

An hour later, green lights rolled in Maggoty's skull. "Gaw, you are such a ma-*hoosive* loser," he said. "Try again."

Sitting cross-legged on her bed, Mallory groaned, shaking her head. "I can't. It's impossible."

"Impossible-shrimpossible. Believe in yourself. Wish upon a star. Dare to dream, you spotty-faced bum-trumpet."

Mallory sucked in a deep breath. She closed her eyes. The frown on her forehead disappeared as she forced herself to relax. In the corners of the room, shadows stirred. Steadying her breathing, she tried to send her thoughts away from her own head. Then stiffened. "NO," she yelped, opening her eyes. "I *can't*."

"*Looooo*-ser," Maggoty scoffed. "What the flaming hoo-ha is so difficult, Smellory? Too knee-wobbly scared to let yourself go, that's your problem. *A-wop-bap-a-looma-a-wop-bam-boo.*"

"You're not making it any easier," Mallory interrupted the skull's singing. She scowled. Much as she hated it,

Maggoty was right. Summoning spirits was easy. Controlling shadows: ditto. But leaving her own body was hard.

"Maggoty told you a bezillion times, everything will be peachy."

"Three. You've told me three times."

"Three, a bezillion. What's the diff? No, shut up. Don't even. Just listen. It. Will. Be. Fine. Your brain will take care of all the breathing and sweating and stuff. Nothing *bad* will happen." Maggoty paused. More quietly, he continued, "Terms and conditions apply. Please ensure your bladder is empty before attempting to shadow walk as damp patches may occur."

"It just doesn't feel right," Mallory said. 'It's not natural."

"Is wiping your bottom natural, Mallsy-Boo? Are toenails natural? Is picking your nose natural?"

"Yes, yes and yes."

"They are, aren't they? Hmm, you've got Maggoty there. Anyhoo, let's try something different. Trust sweet, sweet Maggoty. Close your eyes and listen to his fragrant, kittenish voice."

Mallory closed her eyes.

Maggoty's words took on a sing-song, hypnotic tone.

"Breathe. In-out, in-out. And *reeeeelax*. Feel the shadows. The shadows are part of you. You are part of them. You and the shadows are one…"

Mallory let her awareness slide into the shadows. Even with her eyes closed, she could feel them sliding slowly around the walls, mirroring her thoughts.

"Do you feel them?"

Mallory dropped her head: yes.

"Good. *NOWGETOUTOFYOURFLIPPIN'HEAD.*"

The deafening screech of Maggoty's voice thundered through Mallory's head, driving away any other thoughts. *"Hey!"* she shouted. "You made me jump. I…"

Her words trailed off at the sound of her own voice. It sounded like dust shifting in a tomb. Like the whispers of ghostly librarians.

With a gulp, she opened her eyes, which were no longer her eyes, and saw herself sitting on the bed. Mallory shrieked a spidery shriek and scrambled towards herself on legs of… She stopped and looked down. Her body was made of shadow. She was an impossible, Mallory-shaped patch of darkness.

"I can't feel my legs," she whispered. "What have you done to me?"

"Pff: you said you wanted to learn shadow walking," the skull cackled. "And *ta-dah*: shadow walking. Once again, Maggoty Skull triumphs. You can thank him now or later. Now's best. Maggoty has a thank-you shaped window in his diary. NO... No, Boo. Do NOT dive straight back into your body."

Shadow-Mallory stopped again, fighting down panic. Stepping around herself, light as smoke, she noticed that real-Mallory cast no shadow. It had been detached. She *was* the shadow. As an experiment, she stopped breathing, watching with interest as her real face began turning red.

"Stop that," yelped Maggoty. "Don't look at it. Ignore the old bag of meat 'n' bones. Definitely don't think about being an empty-headed zombie thing with drool dangling off your chin if you don't make it back."

Shadow-Mallory nodded. It sounded like sensible advice.

"Let's have a look at you, then. Give Maggoty a twirl."

Hesitantly, Mallory spun, feeling more confident with every passing second. She caught sight of herself in the mirror: a girl-shaped shadow where no shadow should be. It was ... *extraordinary*. "Err ... thank you, Maggoty," she whispered.

"Frankly, it's an improvement," Maggoty answered. "Look, no bun."

Mallory eyed herself in surprise. The skull was right. Unlike the real Mallory sitting on the bed, her shadow self had dark curls cascading over its shoulders.

"Now: *walkies*," Mallory cackled. "Who's a good girl? Mallory's a good girl. Yes, she is. Take yourself for a whirl, eh? Go explore the world of shadow. Walk the night, as you were born to do."

Mallory was no longer listening. On the bed, her body took another deep breath. Then shadow-Mallory slipped through the wall as if it didn't exist and flitted into the night.

Behind her, another dark figure appeared high on the walls and battlements of Carrion Castle. Hunched, robed and hooded, the shadow of Hellysh Spatzl gazed for a moment at the much smaller shadow-Mallory as she slipped into the night, then it too flitted away in a different direction.

CHAPTER 19

For an instant, panic bubbled in Mallory's chest once more. The ground was a long way beneath her. But gravity didn't apply to shadows. With a thought, she sent herself soaring up above the mismatched Stabbings' rooftops. Fizzing orange street lights grew smaller beneath her.

Above the clouds, far above the city and beneath an endless midnight sky studded with stars, shadow-Mallory twirled, silhouetted by a crescent moon. The freedom was beyond wonder. There was no cold, no fear, no ... Maggoty Skull. Mallory stopped. For the first time since she had picked up the skull, she felt truly alone. And without Maggoty's endlessly distracting jabbering she could hear her own thoughts again. Fear for her parents

suddenly gripped her, harder than ever. In a heartbeat, wonder turned to dread. Where were they? What was Hellysh doing to them? She felt strangely empty too. The skull's yapping was annoying but now silence had fallen she felt almost… Mallory searched for the right word.

Lonely.

Mallory gulped. Could it be? Was it possible that she *missed* him?

She shook her head. No. She couldn't allow herself to start thinking of the bizarre skull as a friend. Maggoty was … well, when you came right down to it, Maggoty was a talking skull. When her normal life returned, he just wouldn't fit. Besides, she told herself, if she managed to break his curse, Maggoty would finally be able to follow Lionel Hadley and go into the light or go wherever it was that ghosts were supposed to go.

Maggoty's curse. She hadn't thought about it much. Despite the skull's confidence, Mallory was certain breaking it wouldn't be anywhere near as simple as a kiss.

And what horrors might be involved in bringing spirits back from the dead?

From the little Maggoty had told her, Mallory knew she had barely scratched the surface of necromancy.

She wondered what else could she do? And what else
would she have to do before she could find her way back
to her old life?

There was only one way to find out.

Mallory willed herself to descend to street level. It
wouldn't be stealing, she told herself.
She would pay Harry
Gizzard for the book
as soon as she had
the money.

But as a shadow, she could sneak into his shop and maybe find a way to take a peek at its pages. Just for a clue of what might lay ahead.

Her shadow skimmed over the cobbles, moving through a world of night, darting from darkness to darkness. Nothing touched her. Rain passed through. Wind failed to shake her curls. She was a creature of the night: cloaked in shade. Wherever there was shadow – which was everywhere – she could be there too. The shadows were where she belonged.

Unseen, she slipped past shop windows and colourful night people who sang and leaned on each other for support – disappearing and reappearing as if the space between shadows didn't exist.

All in all, she decided, shadow walking was pretty snazzy. She was a living ghost. Invisible. Where could it lead her? What secrets could she unravel?

For the first time, Mallory caught a glimmer of what Maggoty had meant when he said that necromancy was power. Cloaked in shadow, nothing could stop her. No door could keep her out. The deepest, most heavily guarded bank vault was hers to explore. She could listen in on the conversations of kings and queens, learn the plans of prime ministers and presidents. And that was just the start of it.

And if she brought Hellysh Spatzl back to life, nothing and no one would be able to stop *her* either.

The thought brought shadow-Mallory to a sharp halt: a shadow against an alley wall, suddenly trembling. Shadow walking and commanding secrets from the dead alone offered endless opportunities for evil. What might Hellysh do if – when – Mallory raised her from the dead?

Mallory's shadow shuddered.

Suddenly it seemed really important to see what was written in her diary.

Her shadow disappeared. Stepping out of darkness further down the road, she glanced into the eyes of a young man lurking in a dark doorway. By the time he blinked, Mallory had gone – already crouched in shadow two jumps down the street.

Ahead was a small alley. Halfway down was Harry Gizzard's House of Curiosities.

Mallory slowed. In the distance a bell chimed twice – two o'clock in the morning.

She hopped from shadow to shadow, closer to the shop. Peering through the tiny window, she saw piles of junk in deep shadow created by the light of a single candle.

"AAAAAAARRRRGHHHH."

A scream sounded from inside the shop: a long, horrible scream of pure terror that spluttered out into a rattling croak. Harry Gizzard staggered from the back room, jerking and thrashing, wrapped in dark shadow. He bounced off the counter. His long nightcap fell as he crashed backwards into a heap of boxes, which collapsed on top of him. Mallory watched his feet kick for a few moments, shudder once, twice, and then go still.

Shadow-Mallory leapt through the window in time to hear a familiar voice – dripping evil – hissing, "The book NOW, little *necromanssssser*."

The darkness that had killed Harry Gizzard melted away and vanished.

Mallory stood rooted to the spot, paralysed by the lingering foulness of Hellysh Spatzl: a spirit that could follow her and watch everything she did – and scare people to death too – but which could not do something as simple as pick up a book.

Back at Carrion Castle, the flesh-and-blood Mallory sat up in bed and screamed.

"Oi, oi! What's going on? Mallory! Come back!" shouted Maggoty Skull. "If you can hear me, come back NOW!"

Fists beat on the door of Harry Gizzard's House of Curiosities. "Oi," someone shouted outside. "You all right, Harry?"

With a last, horrified glance at the dead man on the floor, Mallory's shadow jerked away. At the speed of thought – no longer caring if anyone caught a glimpse of her shadow – she flitted through the door, flickering across cobbles and down dark alleys. All that mattered

was putting distance between herself and Harry Gizzard's House of Curiosities. Faster, faster, until houses and gas lights were a blur, the patch of Mallory-shaped darkness raced through the streets of Stabbings towards Carrion Castle.

Back in her room, Mallory opened her eyes and stared at the wall while her stomach heaved.

"Mallory," gabbled Maggoty Skull. "Mallsy. Mallsy-bum. What happened?"

Mallory drew a shuddering breath, her eyes turned to the skull across the room. "Maggoty," she croaked.

"What *happened*?" the skull repeated.

"Hellysh," Mallory whispered. "Hellysh Spatzl. She ... she *killed* Harry Gizzard."

CHAPTER 20

Green eyes glowed at Mallory. "Umm," said the skull. "What?"

Mallory's reply was cut off by the sound of the door being thrown open and her aunt's wailing voice. *"Darling!"* she cried, bounding across the room in a waft of musty silk and throwing her arms around her niece. "I heard screaming. Oh, let me take you in my arms, you poor, cursed child. Whatever is the matter? Has doom clutched you in its beastly claws?" Dramatically, she threw out one hand and clutched her own forehead. *"No,* wait. I see it now. Mr Lozenge shows me even as we speak. What's that, Mr Lozenge? A dead body, its face twisted in unnatural horror? Is that it?"

Mallory tried pushing her away, and failed. "Err …
actually, yes," she mumbled.

"I *knew* it," sobbed Aunt Lilith, holding her niece
close. "Oh, Mallory. *Murder*! How *could* you? It's the
necromancy. It's happened, hasn't it? You've been
overwhelmed by darkness? Don't fear, you precious,
precious, murderous fiend. Aunt Lilith will stand by you
whatever dreadful crimes you've committed. I shall never
stop believing that somewhere deep inside you there
remains a spark of light. A tiny *glimmer* of humanity."

Finally, Mallory managed to untangle herself from
her weeping aunt. "It's not like that," she insisted.
"Mr Gizzard is dead, but—"

"I expect you can hardly remember what happened,
can you, dear?" Her aunt sat up straighter. "I expect
there was a red mist and the next thing you knew there
was a body lying at your feet. Fight it, Mallory. You *must*
fight it."

"I didn't do it," gasped Mallory. "How could you even
think that?"

"But he had the book you wanted and—"

"I wouldn't *murder* him for it. I wouldn't murder
anyone. Really, Aunt Lilith." Mallory stopped. Her eyes

widened. "The book. Oh."

"Mallory," gasped Aunt Lilith. "What on Earth is going on? If *you* didn't kill Mr Gizzard, who did?"

"Please, Aunt Lilith," said Mallory, scrambling from the bed and reaching for her coat. "I didn't murder anyone. Honestly. Hellysh … the evil spirit … wants me to get the book. I … I didn't understand how far she would go… And I don't know what else she might do." Mallory stopped and gulped. With Harry Gizzard dead, what if someone else took Hellysh's diary? Hellysh would kill again, and again, to get it into Mallory's hands.

Mallory paused, her hand on the door handle. "There's no time to explain. I have to get that book. I have to go now."

"Then I shall come with you," Aunt Lilith said, standing and smoothing her dress. "On the way, you can tell me what is going on."

"And Maggoty," said the skull on the dressing table. "Don't forget Maggoty. The plot thickens and Maggoty likes a nice thick plot."

Mallory leaned against a wall close to Harry Gizzard's

House of Curiosities, breathing heavily, skull tucked beneath her arm. Dawn had yet to arrive but the tiny shop was surrounded by a crowd. A policeman stood outside the door, holding it back. Another was blowing his whistle and shouting at people to go home. People ignored him. A few turned, eyes flickering in the light of flaming torches, looking from the bewigged Maggoty into Mallory's face.

She no longer cared. Let them stare.

"Goodness, what a lot of people." Aunt Lilith looked around. "So, you say the evil spirit killed Mr Gizzard, hmm? It definitely wasn't you in some kind of dark and mystic necromancer trance?"

Too out of breath to speak, Mallory shook her head.

"But I still don't understand *why*, dear. Why would this spirit want such a pointless man dead? What exactly is in this book you're so keen to get your hands on?"

Mallory didn't answer, instead tugging the sleeve of a woman standing next to her. "What ... what's going on?" she panted.

"It's Harry Gizzard. He died under mysterious circumstances," the woman answered, grinning as she bit into a slice of pie.

"I know. I meant, why the crowd?" said Mallory, waving her free hand at all the people.

"Mmmf ... mmmf." The woman swallowed her mouthful. "Ghoulish curiosity," she said, spitting crumbs. "They're bringing out the body in a minute. They say it's a good 'un. Face all twisted up, like *this*." She made a face at Mallory.

"Unmissable event." The man next to her nodded. "You don't clap eyes on a body like that every day."

"Yes, you do, it's Stabbings," said another.

"Well, maybe every other day," the first man admitted. "Still, this corpse is a classic, they say. Eyeballs poppin'

out. Hair standing on end. I mean, you *hear* about hair standing on end but you never really *see* it, do you?"

"Gawping at a corpse," said the woman, stuffing her face again. "Let the good times roll!"

Mallory had heard enough. "We have to get in there," she said. "He – Mr Gizzard – had a book I need."

The first woman spat pie. "Ooh," she squealed. "Poor old Harry's horribly dead with his face all twisted up and you're worried about shopping?" she puffed. "Young people today!"

"*You're* here to gawk at his corpse," Mallory protested.

"A *respectful* gawk," the woman replied, biting into her pie again. "It's … mmmf … it's wha' he would'ff wanted."

Mallory looked up at her aunt. "We have to get inside," she whispered. "We need a distraction."

Aunt Lilith looked down. "Have you got any – you know – *powers* you can use?" She wiggled her fingers magically and lowered her voice to a whisper. "You know: *necromancer* powers."

"Maggoty, have I?" Mallory hissed.

"Summon a thingy from the dark dimensions," said the skull. "Something slobbery with great big pointy teeth. Set it loose on the crowd. Gobble, gobble, gobble. Body

parts everywhere. Screaming, waving of bloody stumps and general scurrying about. That'll distract 'em."

"I can *do* that?" said Mallory.

"We'd have to skip ahead about sixty-eight lessons but sure."

"What does the little skull say?" Aunt Lilith interrupted.

"He says I don't have any powers suitable for this situation," Mallory answered.

"If you'd stolen the book in the first place, like Maggoty said, you wouldn't be in this pickle or jam," the skull continued. "Maggoty hates to say 'I told you so' but... No ... wait ... Maggoty *loves* to say 'I told you so'."

"Perhaps I can help," Aunt Lilith murmured.

"*You?*" said Mallory, her eyes widening. "How can *you* help?" Seeing the look on her aunt's face, she quickly added, "Sorry, that came out wrong."

"I'm not *completely* useless, you know," sniffed Aunt Lilith.

"No. Umm. I meant..."

Holding up a finger to stop Mallory, Aunt Lilith stepped forward, shouting, "Stand aside. Move aside, please. Psychic coming through. Sir, if you could get out of the way. I *am* a psychic."

Mallory stared in disbelief as the crowd parted to let her aunt pass.

The people of Stabbings could spot an interesting scene a mile off and Aunt Lilith was a spectacle unfolding right before their eyes.

"I said, I'm a *psychic*!" bellowed Aunt Lilith, elbowing stragglers out of her path. "There are evil spirits at work here. This shop may very well be a gateway or portal for a demonic infestation. I said, let me through, madam. Do you want to be possessed by gibbering fiends? Oh, I see it's too late for you, sir."

"This should be a laugh," Maggoty muttered.

Shaking her head, Mallory followed her aunt.

CHAPTER 21

"Please, make way," shouted Aunt Lilith, pushing her way to the door of Harry Gizzard's House of Bargains. "Excuse me, officer. I'm needed inside."

A policeman barred her way. "I'm sorry, madam. No one is allowed—"

"I am a highly trained psychic," Aunt Lilith snorted, pushing past him. "If the bungling police force stands any hope of solving this case my help will be needed."

While her aunt argued, Mallory ducked under the policeman's arm. The shop's bell tinkled over her head. Instantly, the stench of horror hit her in a wave that made her stomach heave. She staggered, steadying herself against a heap of boxes, clenching her teeth against the lingering foulness of Hellysh Spatzl.

"Maggoty feels it too," the skull muttered. "*Gross…* Ooooh, that suit is still here! Grab it, Boo. Grab it."

A police inspector looked up from the body on the floor and glared at her. "You can't come in here, young miss," he growled.

The bell rang again. Aunt Lilith entered, standing dramatically in the doorway with her hands on her hips, dark glasses pulled down her nose and black lace floating around her. "I sense *death*," she announced.

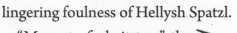

"Well, yes," said the inspector. "There's a body right here on the floor."

"An *unnatural* death," Aunt Lilith went on, her voice dropping into a sinister whisper. "A death caused by supernatural forces."

The inspector stood, wiping his hands on his coat. "Madam," he said, tucking his thumbs into his braces. "I don't know who you are but—"

"Silence," hissed Aunt Lilith, glancing down at the body. Her nose wrinkled. "My spirit guide whispers to me even now. What's that you say, Mr Lozenge? His name? Buzzard? Blizzard? No ... No ... *Gizzard.* Harry Gizzard. The victim's name was Harry Gizzard? Is that what you're trying to tell me, Mr Lozenge?"

Behind the counter a young constable gasped. "How could she have known that?" he croaked.

"This is Harry Gizzard's House of Curiosities," snapped the inspector. "There's a sign above the door."

"I said, be *silent,*" Aunt Lilith insisted. "Foul play, was that, Mr Lozenge? Yes, yes. The victim meddled with forces he could not understand. A book? A red cover. Blood red." She looked up into the younger policeman's eyes. "Mr Lozenge says there is an unholy book here."

The constable glanced beneath the counter and squealed quietly.

"I've had just about enough of this nonsense," snapped the inspector.

"Umm ... sir."

"Madam, I must insist you leave immediately."

"Sir!"

"We are in the middle of an investigation."

"SIR!"

"What is it, Constable Footnote?"

"There is a book, sir," said the constable, holding it up nervously. "We found it by the body and it's ... it's got pictures of goats in. I think it *is* unholy. She ... she really is psychic, sir."

"If you wish to live to see the morning, give it to me," whispered Aunt Lilith, leaning forward to snatch the book from the constable's hands. "It is very dangerous in a mystical way beyond your pitiful understanding. Now, I must expel the evil spirit that infests this shop. Everyone: close your eyes. Whatever happens, do not move."

The constable immediately looked down, closing his eyes and clasping his hands in front of him.

After shooting Aunt Lilith a suspicious glare, the

inspector too closed his eyes. "Make it snappy," he grumbled, adding under his breath, weirdos. Used to let us lock 'em up, but it's all sensitive neighbourhood policing these days. Gah."

"Ooooh, spirits," chanted Aunt Lilith, ignoring the inspector and backing away. She nudged Mallory and jerked her head towards the door. "Oooh, Mr Lozenge," she droned, reaching behind her for the door knob. "Come down unto this dark and dismal shop. Clear it of the dreadful vicious presence that lurks within. Vanquish evil and so on and so forth."

Above her head the doorbells tinkled. "This shop is now clean," said Aunt Lilith. "All part of the service. You're welcome, gentlemen. Come along, Mallory."

Book clasped to her chest, Aunt Lilith turned and scurried into the crowd. With Maggoty under her arm, Mallory followed.

A moment later, the inspector's voice called, "Oi. Come back here. That book's evidence."

Mallory quickened her pace as the crowd closed behind her. Up ahead, her aunt sped up too. "Here," she puffed, passing Hellysh Spatzl's diary to Mallory. "Not *completely* useless, see."

"Stop," her niece replied.

Aunt Lilith stopped, turning towards her under a fizzing street light. "What is it, dear?" she asked.

Awkwardly, Mallory put Maggoty and Hellysh Spatzl's diary on the cobbles, and flung her arms around her aunt. "Thank you," she said, burying her face in velvet.

Aunt Lilith blinked. Gently patting Mallory's head and taking the opportunity to ease out one or two of the pins that were keeping her bun in place, she said, "You're welcome, darling. Now, when we get home we're going to have a very *long* talk."

CHAPTER 22

By the time Mallory and her aunt had made their way through crooked streets back to Carrion Castle, dawn had broken somewhere behind dark clouds. Begging her aunt to be excused the long talk, Mallory fell into bed where – again – her dreams were haunted: the hooded figure in a throne of bones unmoving as fire swirled around it. Shouting people silhouetted against the flames. And shadows.

Always shadows.

She awoke to darkness and distant thunder once more, clutching Hellysh Spatzl's diary in her arms. The storm that had been circling the city for days was closing in but Mallory didn't hear the rumbling sky. Having forgotten

to eat, she chewed on a strand of hair that had escaped her bun while she sat cross-legged on the bed, turning page after page with trembling fingers.

The book felt sinister in her hands, its ragged pages creeping with malice. The words were old-fashioned, too faded to read in places, but after only a few pages Mallory could see Hellysh had been obsessed with human bones. Once, she spent almost an hour squinting at a single page, only to realise that she was looking at instructions on how to make an eye-catching salad bowl using a ribcage.

Mallory turned yet another page. Another hour passed in silence broken only by distant thunder. She lifted her head only once, when the candle sputtered out. With a shrug, she returned to the diary on her lap without stopping to wonder why she no longer needed light to see.

"Is it a five-star, page-turner of a book?" asked Maggoty eventually. "Is it a gasp-worthy, white-knuckle ride of excitement set against a background of dark magicks? Has it got thrills, spills and an oh-so-gorgeous skull as the main character?"

Mallory looked up, shook her head, and returned to reading.

"Any wigs?"

"No." This time she didn't bother looking up.

"Sounds awful," sighed Maggoty. "What's the point of a book with no gorgeous skull wearing smashing wigs? *Boring.*"

Mallory turned another page, her sense of dread deepening. With every page her questions were being answered, pointing the way to her own future. This was what it meant to be a necromancer. Among creepy diary entries, Hellysh had scrawled notes, including lists of creatures that existed in the dead dimensions – demons, ghouls, tortured spirits and worse – and how they could be summoned to spread mayhem. Mallory found step-by-step instructions on how to create vampires; curses for everything from hair loss to agonising pain; recipes for deadly poisons; a how-to guide on 'Maykyng thee Most of Shadow Walkyng', which included goosebumping directions on moving between the worlds of the living and the dead. At the centre of it all was the power Mallory could feel burning in her stomach. The mysterious magic of necromancy was an essential ingredient in every curse, summons and potion. Hellysh Spatzl's book detailed hundreds of ways it could be used.

Mallory didn't want to learn any of them.

Shivering with disgust, she told herself once more that she would never use necromancy again as soon as her parents returned and forced herself to turn yet another page.

"Oh." The strand of hair dropped from her mouth. She peered closer, lifting the book to her eyes and running a finger across words as she read them. "This page seems to be about your curse, Maggoty."

Green lights flared in the skull. "Woo," the skull yelped. "Whatsitsay? Whatsitsay? Sweet cherry lips, right? Pucker up, Mallsy-Boo. Give Maggoty your best smooch. Horrible, *yes*. But somehow, Maggoty will just have to get through the whole ghastly experience. Try not to drool, eh, spotty? And keep your hands to yourself."

"Shush," said Mallory. "There's nothing about kissing here..." Her words trailed off. Her already pale face turned two shades paler.

"What?" screeched the skull. "Now is not the time for dramatic pauses, Boo. Tell Maggoty. Tell, tell, tell, tell, tell, tell, tell."

"All right, all right. Shut up for once and listen."

Taking a deep breath, Mallory read aloud.

Thee Spyrit Pryson: An Most Amusyng Curse of Mine Own Invenchun

Thys curse do mayke a pryson or jayl for thee soul of the victim, leaving the cursèd one trapped for all of tyme ytself, and completely powerless. Nothyng, not eeven magick, can escaype. The Necromancer may Bind Thee vyctim's spiryt withyn any object but theyre own Skull do mayke an attractive home decoration and hys or hyr endless wayling torment wyll gyve hours of Entertainmynt. Eesy to creyate by even an apprentyce thys curse ys so strong even I, the grate Hellysh Spatzl, cannot brayke it. Only Death and a grate sacrifice can brayke it.

Mallory turned to the next page and then turned back again. "There's instructions on how to perform the curse but nothing else on how it can be undone," she said with a groan.

Voice wobbling, Maggoty said, "Nothing? Not even a teeny ickle clue?"

"It just says only death could break it," Mallory repeated, frowning. "And a sacrifice. But you're already dead. What does that mean?"

"Err ... perhaps kill Maggoty all over again. Try stabbing him. A pointy stick through an eye socket should do the trick."

"No," said Mallory gently. "That would be too easy."

"Eeeek! Maggoty's stuck inside his skull for ever? Is that what we're saying now? 'Cos if that's what we're saying then – y'know – *gulp*."

Getting off the bed, Mallory crossed to the dressing table and picked up the skull. She brought it up so she could look deep into the eye sockets where green lights blinked. "I'm sorry, Maggoty," she whispered. "Truly. If ... if makes any difference I'm ... well ... I'm glad you'll have to stay a little bit longer."

The lights in Maggoty's eye sockets blinked again.

"What, like we're friends?" he squeaked.

Mallory nodded gently, her forehead touching bone. "I think ... yes ... that's what we are," she said. "And there has to be a way. There's *always* a way. After I've found my parents, I'll do whatever I can to break your curse, whatever sacrifice it takes."

"You will?"

"Yes."

"Promise?"

"Mmm hmm."

"No backsies?"

Mallory nodded again. "Uh huh," she murmured. "No backsies."

Maggoty's voice brightened. "Well, all *riiiight*. I suppose Maggoty doesn't have to let Mallory kiss him, at least. Every cloud has a single lime in, eh?"

Mallory rolled her eyes. "It's 'silver lining'."

"*Whaaaat?* Ever seen a cloud with a silver lining? No. Pff. It's definitely every cloud has a single lime in."

"No, really, it's silver li—"

"Whatevs," Maggoty interrupted. "Bored of that now. So, Mallory's going to break the curse, and Maggoty and Mallory are friends. Yay! Let's do friend stuff. Pyjamas!

Popcorn! Pillow fights! Oooh, would you like Maggoty to do something with your hair? 'Cos – just between us friends – *someone* needs to."

Mallory reached up to pat her bun. "Umm ... no. No, thank you. Anyway, there's no time for any of that. Hellysh, remember?"

"Oh, yaas, Hellysh," grumped Maggoty. "That horrible old bottom-nibbler."

"Getting my parents back is important to me, so it should be important to you too," Mallory said softly, making her way back to the bed and setting the skull down beside her. "That's how the friend thing works."

"Yeah, but Hellysh. *Bleurgh*. Is it too late to not be friends again?"

"Yes. Now be quiet."

Mallory turned another page. Time passed in darkness lit only by the glow of Maggoty's eyes.

"Here," Mallory hissed, after a while. She jabbed a finger at the page. "*How to Rayse the Ded*. Listen: 'The walking ded mayke excellent servants. To clothe a spyrit in flesh, start with the bones. Any part of thee skellyton wyll do, and thys spell wyll give any shambling corpse a luverly withered, dryed-up look.' She says it helps strike

an extra note of terror if they have bits of skin falling off."

"She's not wrong, is she?" Maggoty said. "A dried-up, dangling eyeball also adds a touch of class."

"Skin falling off," Mallory repeated, with a shiver. She stopped, a frown creasing her forehead. "What I don't understand is why does Hellysh even want to come back if she's going to be a dried-up, soulless, broken, shuffling thing?"

Maggoty thought about it. "Maybe she wants to work as a geography teacher," he suggested.

Mallory didn't reply. The only sound she made was a half-gasp, half-sob of sudden understanding.

"Oi, what's happening to your face, Boo? It's giving Maggoty the heebie-jeebies. Stop it. Stop it this instant."

Mallory ignored him. She'd been cheated. Conned. Fooled.

As hope died, a pit opened in her stomach. She read the words again silently. They hadn't changed – *Thys spell wyll give any shambling corpse a luverly withered, dryed-up look.*

Tears spilled from her eyes. It wasn't just Hellysh who would come back as a shambling husk. This was what the wicked old necromancer had promised when she had

said Mallory could bring her parents back. It had been the truth, but a twisty, cruel kind of truth. Certainly not the *whole* truth. "My parents would be like that too?" she choked. "If … if … I brought them back. Undead. Not really alive at all. Not properly."

"Oh, that. Ummm … yeah. Uh huh," said the skull, his voice more gentle than usual. "Did Maggoty not say? However much power you put into them, the stench of the grave clings, sort of thing. It's all a bit icky and people notice. 'Oh, look,' they'll say. 'Here come the Vayles. Watch your brain or they'll be picking it out their teeth.'"

"There's … there's … no other way?" Mallory asked.

"Not that Maggoty knows of," said the skull.

Desperately, Mallory flicked through the remaining pages of Hellysh's diary, already knowing she would find nothing.

And nothing was exactly what she found. Just grim diary entries and a recipe for gingerbread houses.

This was the ritual Hellysh wanted her to perform.

She squeezed her eyes shut, shuddering. Opening them, she blinked tears. Deep down she had known that it was too good to be true. Her parents couldn't come back. Not the way she wanted them. Not ever.

It made no difference. Mallory gritted her teeth. Her ma and da's spirits were still trapped and if she didn't obey Hellysh, who knew what horrors she would inflict on them? Returning to the book, she turned back pages and croaked, "It says here I have to find her bones. Any idea where to start looking?"

The skull managed to look as though it was shrugging. "The ghosties would know but ... err ... maybe we should – y'know – revisit this plan, Boo?" he said. "All right, Hellysh will come back all manky and dribbly but she'll still have some of her power. Enough to be a total pain in the bum."

Mallory grunted, reading the rest of the instructions. She stopped, gasping and pushed the book away from her in disgust. "No," she said. "Just no. Absolutely not. It says here that the necromancer must tear the spirit of life from a victim and use its energy to create new flesh for the dead."

"Brrr, that is a bit extreme," Maggoty agreed. "Maggoty did say Hellysh had bits of her mechanism gone wonky…"

Maggoty stopped, watching Mallory's shoulders heave. The brief flicker of almost-hope had burned out again. If

saving her parents meant taking someone else's life then they really were lost.

"Yeeeches, Mallsy. Don't cry," he squealed. "There, there, sort of thing. Your great pal Maggoty is here. Look: wig. *Huzzah*."

"It *won't* be all right. *Nothing* will ever be all right again." Mallory put her face in her hands, tears falling between her fingers. "My ma and da are trapped for ever in some … some … ho-horrible dead dimension with H-Hellysh. I … I can't do it, Muh-Muh-Maggoty. I can't."

A gentle knocking came from the door. "Mallory." Aunt Lilith's voice. "Are you awake, darling?"

CHAPTER 23

Without waiting for an answer, Aunt Lilith pushed the door open. "Look, I made mashed potatoes," she said, peering around the door. "At least I think it's mashed potatoes. But who really understands the ways of potatoes? Oh, Mallory. You're *crying*."

In a soft flurry of velvet, Aunt Lilith let the tray she was carrying clatter to the floor and crossed to the bed.

Mallory leaned into her aunt's chest as arms circled her.

Her parents were gone.

For *ever*.

Mallory sobbed.

"Whatever is the matter, darling?" Aunt Lilith

murmured when Mallory's tears subsided a little. "Is this about you being an evil crone again?"

Lifting her head, Mallory nodded.

"Oh dear. Maybe it's time we had that little talk, hmm?"

Sniffing back tears, her voice breaking, Mallory nodded a second time. It didn't matter now what her aunt knew. Nothing mattered. Nothing would ever matter again.

Her voice breaking, Mallory told her aunt everything. She told her about her parents. Maggoty. And mostly, she told her about Hellysh Spatzl. At the end, she sat up, straightening her shoulders. "I was going to do it too," she said in a small voice. "I was going to bring her back to life. I *am* an evil crone."

"*Wicked,*" Maggoty corrected. "Mischievous. A little bit naughty. But not the 'E' word. Never the 'E' word, Boopsy. Ooh, Boopsy. Maggoty likes that. Can—"

"No, you cannot call me Boopsy," Mallory snapped.

Seeing her aunt blinking in confusion, she added, "Umm … sorry, Aunt Lilith. It's … uh … you know." She waved a hand at the skull, allowing a whisper of necromancy to leak from her fingertips.

Aunt Lilith whimpered, watching the skull's eyes brighten.

One flashed on and off in a wink. "Wotcha," said Maggoty. "Can't be in the slightest bit bothered to remember your name but touch the wig again and there will be blood. *Your* blood. Get it?"

"Just ignore him," said Mallory, sniffing again and giving Maggoty a stern look. "He says things like that but he can't actually do anything because he's just ... a ... skull."

"Umm, yes ... yes," said Aunt Lilith. "Perhaps you should put it back where you found it, hmm?"

Maggoty growled.

"Or perhaps not," said Aunt Lilith hurriedly. Turning back to her niece, she seemed to put the talking skull out of her mind. "So, let me get this right, Mallory. You're saying you were going to dig up the bones of a five-hundred-year-old, evil-dead necromancer and give flesh to this ... this ... Helen Pretzl—"

"Hellysh Spatzl," Mallory interrupted.

Aunt Lilith's nose wrinkled in disgust. She waved a hand. "Hellysh Spatzl," she corrected herself. "Who murdered your parents, imprisoned their spirits and ... ahh ... is blackmailing you into bringing her back to life. Is that what you're saying? Have I got that right, darling?"

Mallory nodded.

"You can *do* that?"

"Raise the dead? Yes. It's pretty much what necromancy is all about. The book gives instructions."

"Umm … I understand that you're on a journey of self-discovery, Mallory," Aunt Lilith murmured, "but a new hair-do would have been a much better idea."

"I told you, I had no choice," said Mallory. Her shadow began pacing the walls, twisting its hands together. "But I can't do it. Not if it means killing someone."

She stopped and looked up at her aunt guiltily. "Umm … while we're talking I … well … I wanted you to know this isn't the *real* me. Meddling with death. I … I don't usually tell people this but … but … I like books about ponies." Mallory blushed and looked down again. "I'm … I'm sorry. I'm sorry I've been nothing but trouble—"

Her aunt silenced her with a finger held aloft. "You poor dear lambkin," she said. "It all sounds awful. I had no idea things were so bad."

"Maggoty knew," said the skull, a shudder in its voice. "Ponies. *Ugh.*"

"But, darling," her aunt sighed. Patting her niece's hair,

she started pulling out the pins that kept Mallory's bun in place. Curls began falling to her shoulders as her aunt continued. "Just out of interest – and Aunty Lilith isn't saying you should do it, because it all sounds a teeny bit like trafficking with the forces of darkness – but just out of interest why would you have to kill anyone to perform this … ahh .. ritual?"

Mallory sat up, blinking. "What?"

"I know you think I'm a big old silly, dear, but if it's a lot of psychic energy you need then why would you take it all from just *one* person? I expect it's a ghastly human sacrifice thing, isn't it?"

While Mallory stared at her aunt, open-mouthed, Maggoty choked. "*Gah*. Skinny aunt whatserface is right," he finally managed to splutter. "You could take a little bit from ten people. Or a tiny bit from a hundred. Or even less from … ooh … say, five hundred people."

"The Grand Séance," Mallory gasped. "If I did it at the Grand Séance—"

"Now, now, sweetheart," her aunt interrupted. "People will expect a show, but raising the corpse of some foul necromancer who's been rotting in her grave for five hundred years might not give the best impression of

modern psychics, don't you think?"

Mallory wasn't listening. Somewhere in the back of her mind she could sense the beginnings of an idea. She tried to catch it but it slipped away. Something to do with the book. With Maggoty. With *bones*. "Aunt Lilith," she said slowly, interrupting her aunt who was still babbling on about the Grand Séance. "Would you help me?"

"Help you? Oh, poppet." Her aunt clapped her hands, leaving half of Mallory's hair down and the other half still tied up in the wreckage of its bun. "Of course. Should we ... should we ask spirits for guidance at this difficult time?"

Mallory looked up at her aunt. "Asking the spirits wasn't what I had in mind, but why not? Perhaps you could do a card reading?"

Her aunt blinked. *"Really?"* she said.

"Really," Mallory said, nodding.

Her aunt dipped a hand into a pocket for the deck of cards she carried everywhere. Handling them as if they were made of glass, she said, "You're sure?"

Mallory nodded. Her shadow was still and quiet now.

"But you know I'm not really psychic, dear."

Mallory looked into her aunt's violet eyes, which

looked so much like the eyes of her mother. "Maybe the spirits just talk to you more quietly," she said.

"Do you think so?"

Mallory shrugged. "You were right about the Nonger. And Mr Gizzard's twisted-up corpse."

"If you think it will help." Aunt Lilith raised her eyes to the ceiling. "Oh, Mr Lozenge—" she began, shuffling.

"No," said Mallory. "I'd like your advice, not Mr Lozenge's."

"Very well," said Aunt Lilith, shuffling again.

A card flew from the deck and landed face up in front of Mallory: a young girl sitting at a table behind upside-down cups.

"Which card is it?" asked Mallory, peering at it curiously.

"Anita Pea," said her aunt softly.

"I bet you do," Maggoty chipped in. "It's all that nasty tea you drink."

Mallory cuffed the skull gently, knocking his wig over one eye socket.

Aunt Lilith glanced at the skull, shuddered, then pointed to the card. "Anita Pea hides her pea under one of these cups. People think they know where the pea will end up when she switches the cups around, but Anita is a trickster. Her pea always shows up where it's least expected."

It wasn't necromancy. But it felt right. And it chimed exactly with the idea that was starting to grow in Mallory's mind.

The idea she hardly dared think about.

Just in case Hellysh Spatzl could read her thoughts too.

Aunt Lilith shuffled again. "Let's see what else the cards have to say."

"Let's not," said Mallory, laying her hand over the card. "I think that's exactly what I needed to hear. Anita Pea, hmm?"

"Better go quick or you'll wet yourself," giggled the skull. "Oh, Maggoty, you are an absolute *scream*."

Mallory rolled her eyes, sighing. "Yes," she said, her voice brighter now. "That was very interesting. Do you trust me, Aunt Lilith?"

Her aunt blinked. "Umm ... yes. Yes. I suppose I have to, don't I? That's part of the family thing, isn't it?"

Mallory smiled. "Thank you. The Grand Séance is tomorrow night. Would you... Can I leave all the arrangements to you? There's something I need to do."

"You're going through with it, then?" Aunt Lilith gulped. "You're actually going to bring the dead back from the grave?"

Mallory looked around at her bedroom's deep shadows, feeling the spiteful presence of Hellysh Spatzl lurking. Choosing her words carefully, she said loudly, "Tomorrow night I am going to weave necromancy the world has not seen in centuries."

Only Mallory heard Hellysh's distant, triumphant cackle of triumph.

"But ... but ... *Mallory*," squealed her aunt.

Mallory looked up directly into her eyes. Pricks of purple magic sparkled in her own. She smiled. "Please, Aunt Lilith. We'll need a stage. Lights. Everything. Make it big. Make it spooky. Make it *spectacular*."

Mallory paused for a second. Then, her voice hopeful, she said, "Oh, and, Aunt Lilith?"

"Yes, darling?"

"Do you have a spade I could borrow?"

CHAPTER 24

Mallory trailed her hand over gravestones, following the bent ghost of an old gravedigger through the cemetery. A crow on a gravestone tilted its head, watching as she passed. "Here, miss," the ghost wheezed, lifting a ghostly lamp over a headstone so old it was little more than a crumbling nub of moss poking up from a grassy mound surrounded by ankle-clinging mist. "Here lie the bones of the cursed Hellysh Spatzl."

"Thank you, Mr Grumple," said Mallory, setting Maggoty down on another nearby gravestone, and leaning on the spade her aunt had found. "I hope the afterlife is treating you well."

In the distance, thunder growled.

"Can't complain," wheezed the ghost. "I keeps meself busy. Sometimes I likes to touch people on the back of the neck with freezing, deathly fingers. But not very often. You can overdo that sort of thing."

"Well, don't let us keep you if you've got places to haunt," said Mallory.

The ghost ignored her, lifting his lamp a little higher and waving it in the direction of more graves. "If you has an interest in goings-on of an historical nature, Stabbings Cemetery is proud to be the final resting place of the area's most well-known personalities. I could give you a tour, if you likes. We got murderers, blackmailers, muggers and thieves, rascals, ruffians: the lot. Over there's the grave of old Nanna Spangler, the Stabbings Strangler. Ten husbands. Every one of them ... currrruggh."

The gravedigger made a choking sound and ran a fingernail across his throat.

"Thank you, that's a very ... err ... interesting story, Mr Grumple," said Mallory.

"She weren't the worst of them, though," the ghost shivered. "Over there by the tree is Rodney 'The Eel'..."

"*Really*, thank you," said Mallory firmly. "Just this grave is fine."

Once again, the ghost of Mr Grumple paid no attention. Peering down at Hellysh's grave, he continued, "Ah, yes, old Hellysh," he whispered. "I was there when the mob burned her, you know. Back in the days when Stabbings was just a little village near the old castle. Flaming torches, there was. Pitchforks. She done things what'd make your teeth shrivel. Cursed old Jinkin's pig. Then there was all the undead lurching about the village. Plus the unpleasantness with her servant ... Matthew something or other. They say she cut his head right off. He was an annoying little git, of course, but—"

"*Oi!*" shrieked Maggoty. "You wonky old twazzock. I'll—"

"Mr Grumple," Mallory interrupted before Maggoty could get properly started. "If you don't mind, I'm

quite busy."

"When the villagers broke down the door of Carrion Castle, they found her sitting cool as you like. In a great big chair made of bones."

"Mr Grumple!"

"Burned up lovely, though," said the dead gravedigger. "Your witches do make a nice warm fire. I'll give 'em that."

"I really must get on. I haven't got all night."

"Funny thing, though," said Mr Grumple, putting his head to one side. "She never said a word. Never moved. Just sat there while they tied her up, and not even a whimper when she burned."

'Err ... Malls," said Maggoty Skull.

"Shush, Maggoty."

Mr Grumple shrugged and gave Mallory a grin. "I'll be off, then, miss," he finished, lifting his ghostly lamp and floating away into the night. Over his shoulder, he called back, "Good luck with all your ghoulish endeavours, and when the time comes for your own funeral, remember to choose Stabbings Cemetery. A wretched midnight grave robber such as yourself will feel right at home."

Mallory clutched her spade as the ghost faded.

"Well, here we are," chirped Maggoty brightly. "Isn't

this jolly? Mist curling around your ankles. Distant thunder. Spade at the ready to commit the unspeakable crime of grave robbing. Maggoty approves. Oh. One teeny-weeny problemette, Mallsy Boo."

"Yes," said Mallory. "I know."

"You *know*?"

Mallory shrugged calmly. "Something has been bothering me about Hellysh since we went to her old chambers. At first I thought it was just the whole evil, hissing crone thing. But then you taught me shadow walking and I started to think. Finding out she couldn't come back properly was the last piece of the puzzle. It's obvious when you really think about it. She's never appeared to me like a ghost would. Always stayed hidden. Always in the shadows. And she wouldn't want to come back without all her horrible powers. Even my dreams have been trying to tell me the same thing. She didn't put up a fight because she wasn't there. When they found her, her spirit was away shadow walking. They only burned her body. Hellysh Spatzl isn't a ghost, is she? She's just stuck in shadow. And she's been following me around since I got here. Probably listening to us right now. So we shouldn't talk about it."

"She isn't *proper* dead," Maggoty hissed.

"It doesn't change anything," said Mallory, hefting the spade.

"Ha ha ha HA," chuckled Maggoty. "Yeah, it changes nothing. Oh, except when you bring her back, Hellysh won't be a dangly eyeballs, comedy zombie thing mumbling about brains and dropping skin on the carpets. No. 'Cos she never really died, did she? So, you – Mallsy-Wallsy-doo-be-doo-be-doo-de-huuuuuge-pranny – will just be reattaching the shadow of history's most powerful necromancer to a fully alive and not even a little bit undead, living, breathing Hellysh."

"It changes nothing," Mallory insisted, jamming her spade into the dirt with a *shh-runch* sound.

"And that would be very, *very* dangerous, is what Maggoty is saying."

"We shouldn't talk about it," Mallory repeated. With a rattle of stones, she tossed a spadeful of dirt over her shoulder.

"Uh huh. Not talking about it. Okey dokey, pig in a pokey. You're doing that all wrong, by the way. Jam the spade in, use your foot to force it down, lever up the dirt and swing it to the side in one easy movement. Singing a

jaunty grave-robber tune will make the time pass quicker. Maggoty's favourite was always 'She's Got Eyeballs Full of Worms'. Join in when you're ready: *Ooooh, she once had eyes like summer skies, but now they're full of worms...*"

"Shhh," said Mallory. "This is disgusting enough. You're not helping."

"Loosen up, Boo. If you absolutely have to bring a hideous necromancer back to life, you might as well have a bit of fun while you're at it."

Pressing her lips together in determination, Mallory forced the spade into the dirt again.

Shh-runch.

Shh-runch.

"Malls. Mallsy-Ballsy-Boooo-di-Buttcrack."

"Mallory."

The moon sailed across a sky of billowing clouds. Mallory didn't answer. She just dug.

At last, her spade hit wood. In silence, she cleared the lid of the coffin, which was a simple, nailed-together box, its wood mostly rotten. She levered it open with the spade. Half the lid came away with a graveyard creak, which Mallory thought was appropriate in the circumstances.

Bending, Mallory reached in and lifted the skull of

Hellysh Spatzl. Bone glowed white in the moonlight. Dark eye sockets glared at her as if it was all her fault. A few strands of burned hair clung to it for a few seconds and then dropped out and fell into the mist. "Funny how things change," Mallory muttered. "A week ago, I'd have screamed. Now, I have enough skulls to juggle with." Tossing the skull up and catching it, she sighed. "This one doesn't look all that scary."

"Oh, she'll be a *lot* scarier with flesh on her bones," said Maggoty.

The skull paused. Bright green sparks of light in his eye sockets flicked from side to side as if checking the coast was clear. "About now is the time to be asking yourself if you should – y'know – *not* do this, Mallory," he whispered. Maggoty's voice dropped even lower. "She'll turn on you, you know. When you're no longer useful. She won't want to share the spotlight with another necromancer."

Mallory glanced over at him. "My parents," she reminded him quietly. "I can't just forget about them, Maggoty. I have to do *something*. She looked up at the lightening sky. "And we've run out of time. The Grand Séance is tonight."

CHAPTER 25

NEWS OF THE WEIRD
This Week's Messages From Beyond the Grave

GRAND SÉANCE

Join us for an *EXTRAVAGANZA* of ghostly thrills at Carrion Castle. Experience the *AMAZING* supernatural skills of

MALLORY VAYLE.

Seeing is *BELIEVING*, and you won't believe what you see!

Thunder rocked Carrion Castle. Lightning crackled, illuminating rain-swollen clouds from within. As the hidden sun set and true darkness fell, Mallory woke to churning skies. Wind howled around Carrion Castle's broken stones, tugging dead leaves of ivy from the walls and sending bats swirling around turrets. Rain spackled against the window.

"Maggoty!" she gasped, accelerating from half-asleep to full panic in less than a second. "The Grand Séance! I'm not ready."

Scrambling out of bed, she scurried to the dressing table and stared into the cracked mirror. Pushing curls out of her eyes, she looked down at her crumpled, mud-spattered clothes. "Oh, I'm dressed," she mumbled, voice still fuzzy with sleep. Fragments of the morning settled into her head. Mostly it had been about chairs. Mostly her aunt yelling at people about chairs, then her aunt yelling at *her* about chairs. Chairs, Mallory had learned at high volume, were easy enough to find if you wanted to throw a small dinner party but getting five hundred chairs at short notice wasn't as simple as people often thought.

Chairs, and the finding of chairs, had only held

Mallory's attention for so long, and she had escaped to her room, telling her aunt she needed to rest before the Grand Séance began. Sleep had not been easy to find either, though, with all the banging and her aunt's screeching below in the great hall of Carrion Castle. Now, she had things to do. Important things. *Horrible* things. The ritual, she reminded herself. Yes, she had to perform brain-meltingly grim necromancy.

"Cool your boots, Boo," said the skull. "It's only just gone dusk."

The castle was quiet. Thunder and wind the only sounds. Next to the muddy, bare skull of Hellysh Spatzl on the dressing table, Maggoty Skull grinned a skull grin. "Not nice leaving Maggoty with Hellysh's skull all day," he sniffed. "Bleeee-urgh: skulls. *Ick.*"

Mallory gazed at herself, brushing off dried mud and smoothing out the wrinkles in her black dress – the same dress she'd worn to her parents' funeral. That done, she began twisting her hair back into its bun. Jamming pins into it, she glanced down, her eyes darting from Maggoty to Hellysh Spatzl's skull. One eyebrow raised. Except for a few splatters of grave muck and a wig, the two were identical.

"Huh. Don't look at Maggoty like that. There are skulls and there are skulls. Maggoty Skull is *gorgeous*. Hellysh Spatzl's skull would give anyone the willies. It's a willy-giving skull if ever Maggoty saw one."

Over gusting wind, Mallory heard the great door of Carrion Castle boom. Her stomach twisted with nerves as she stuck the last hairpin into place. People were starting to arrive. It was almost time.

She stared into the mirror, murmuring, "I am really, really, *really* not ready for this."

"Mallsy-bum. Boo…"

"I know what you're going to say," Mallory interrupted without taking her eyes off the mirror. "Blah, blah, blah, Hellysh is evil. Blah, blah, don't do it. Probably something about walruses too. Am I right?"

"Yes, well, Maggoty stands by the walrus plan," sniffed the skull. "It was a doozy. One of Maggoty's best."

Mallory opened her mouth to speak. Before she could, the skull continued. "But that wasn't what Maggoty was going to say. Maggoty had a whole speech worked out. Been writing it all day."

Mallory glanced down again. "Really? What were you going to say?"

"The moment's gone now," said the skull, sounding sulky. "Mallory killed it."

Mallory sighed. "We both know you're going to say it, because you never can shut up. So just get on with it."

"Hurrumph. Yes, Maggoty said 'hurrumph'. He meant it to sting too."

"Maggoty!"

"Oh, all right. Keep your badly styled hair on," huffed the skull. "It looks awful, by the way."

"For crying out loud. Maggoty!"

"All right. Touchy, touchy." The skull paused. "All right, then: Maggoty's big speech. Ready? *Good.* So Maggoty was going to say … *cough … cough…* Wait for silence… Aaaaand… Good evening. It's great to see so many of you here. On this very special occasion Maggoty would like to say thank you for this incredible award. Obviously, Maggoty totally deserves it but it means so much to be named Wig Wearer of the Year…"

The skull stopped. "Wait. Wrong speech. Just a second."

Mallory sighed, rolling her eyes.

"Oh, yes, here we are," the skull went on. "So, Maggoty wanted to say that raising Hellysh from the dead is bonkersly stupid…"

"You said you weren't going to—"

"Don't interrupt," huffed the skull. "Anyhoo, no matter how stupid – no, *idiotic* – raising Hellysh from the dead might be, Maggoty wants you to know, Mallory Bumface Vayle, that Maggoty believes in you. Obviously, he also believes you're a ma-*hoosive* nong, but if you absolutely have to do something so mind-bendingly stupid, do it with style, eh? Do it with panache. Do it *hard*, Boo. Show 'em what a bum-kicking, dark and powerful nong you are. Give 'em a show they'll be talking about for years. Sprinkle some *glitter* on it. Give 'em a *show*."

A few seconds earlier, Mallory wouldn't have believed it possible, but she felt a smile curve her mouth. "Thank you, Maggoty."

"Mallory, *Mallory*," her aunt called, pushing open the door without knocking. "People are sitting down, darling. Already. I've been rushed off my feet..." She stepped back, her face falling at the sight of Mallory's plain dress and the bun. "Darling, you *promised*. Oh, drat it. There's no time to fix it now but really, dear, you might've made an effort."

She stopped for a moment, peering at her niece. "Umm ... will ... will everything be all right, Mallory?"

she continued, worried. "I mean, you're absolutely sure no one is going to die? I'd have to give people their money back. I do trust you. Of course, I do. But poor Aunt Lilith is just a teensy bit bothered that—"

"Aunt Lilith?"

"Yes, darling."

With a confidence she did not feel, Mallory smiled. "Everything is going to be fine," she said.

"If you say so, dear," her aunt replied, unconvinced. "Well, if you're absolutely positive everything is tickety-boo, I'll leave you to get ready. Someone has to show people to their seats, I suppose. Do at least let your hair down, dearest."

Her aunt turned to go.

"*Wait*. Aunt Lilith?"

"Yes, darling?"

Mallory pushed a skull into her aunt's hands. "Would you take Maggoty down with you? Give him a front row seat."

Her aunt took the skull gingerly, her nose wrinkling. "Could we at least leave the wig off? Just for tonight?" she said.

"Could we at least pull her lungs out and beat her to

death with them? Just for tonight?" said Maggoty.

Mallory's smiled widened. "No," she told her aunt. "He wouldn't like that."

"Very well," Aunt Lilith sniffed, keeping Maggoty at arm's length. "Though it will ruin the atmosphere I've been trying to create. I suppose I'll see you down there, then. Five minutes?"

"Five minutes," Mallory confirmed, with a gulp. She closed the door, leaned against it and took a deep breath.

Alone.

Crossing back to the mirror she stared at herself. A girl in a simple black funeral dress stared back. Her aunt was right, she decided. At five shillings a ticket the audience deserved someone who looked at least a little bit mystical.

With another sigh, she pulled the pins from her bun again, and shook her head. Curls dropped to her shoulders. Tucking Hellysh Spatzl's skull under one arm, she picked up the old necromancer's diary and took a last look in the mirror. She had the skull and the book and a plan. Everything she needed. Now she had to face a crowd of people and perform a hideous act of darkest necromancy.

"Between you and me," she whispered to the girl who

stared back at her, "*now* I'm ready. Let's show 'em what a bum-kicking, dark and powerful nong you are."

A mixture of necromancy and excitement sizzled in her stomach.

She smiled at herself.

Her parents were not coming back from the grave, but whatever else happened, tonight they would be freed from Hellysh Spatzl's ghastly clutches.

CHAPTER 26

Making her way down a corridor lined with peeling wallpaper, Mallory tossed Hellysh's skull up and down in her spare hand. Pushing down a knee-wobbling wave of nerves, she reached into the mysterious well of necromancy deep inside. No one was looking at her, but if they had they might have noticed tiny stars of purple twinkling deep, deep within her eyes. They might have seen the thin veins under Mallory's skin turn dark.

Stopping in the shadows at the top of the grand staircase, listening to thunder growl, she looked down.

The great hall of Carrion Castle was packed with people from across the city, crowded in for an evening of spooky thrills and ghostly fun. Jostling each other, they

peered around at the decrepit but still impressive room, elbowing each other for space. Mallory was impressed. Aunt Lilith seemed to have begged, borrowed or stolen every chair in Stabbings and packed the vast hall to bursting. From above, the crowd looked like a sea of bonnets and hats, umbrellas and wet overcoats. Curls of steam rose from clothes that were drying under the heat of a hundred candles in the chandelier. Cobwebs billowed every time the door opened to let in more people.

Mallory nodded to herself. Her aunt really was very good at creating a scene. Carrion Castle looked exactly like the kind of place where supernatural events unfolded.

A thunderclap shuddered the castle to its foundations. Dust and plaster rained from the ceiling on to the audience below. At the sound of squeals and giggling shrieks, Mallory felt her nerves begin to steady before a now familiar stench filled her nostrils. Maggots writhed in her stomach.

"Dooo it," hissed Hellysh's voice behind her. "Do it *nowww*. Make me *live*."

Mallory didn't bother looking round, already knowing she would see only shadow. Instead, she shook her head. "Soon," she replied. "I promised my aunt a show first."

Hellysh hissed and spat like a pan boiling over on the stove while the last few stragglers made their way to their seats.

Mallory ignored her. "Sprinkle some glitter on it," she murmured to herself.

Leaning against the banister at the top of Carrion Castle's sweeping staircase, she whispered under her breath. Unseen, poltergeists obeyed her Voice, flitting through the grand entrance hall to slam the great castle doors.

BOOOOOM.

"Speak, spirits. And keep it spooky," Mallory whispered, using her Voice.

Speak … make yourself known … spooky … give 'em a show…

Disembodied voices filled the hall: the moans and whispers of ghosts, louder and louder. The corners of Mallory's mouth twitched. This part of the evening, she decided, might actually turn out to be fun. Things had changed in the few days she had been at Carrion Castle, she thought to herself. The Mallory who had arrived would have run screaming at the thought of standing in front of all these people and showing off her strange

talents. Now, she no longer cared what they thought.

None of it mattered.

All that mattered was that she would soon be reunited with her ma and da.

Ghosts groaned. One – more dramatic than the others – gave an excellent performance, Mallory thought; screaming a horrible, bloody scream that gurgled on and on. People sat up in their chairs, heads craning to see where the noise was coming from. A few whimpered quietly. Again, Mallory smiled, scanning the view below.

The hall was filled with shadow.

And all of it belonged to her.

From the stage, her aunt looked up, spotting her.

Mallory gave her a wink, then stepped back. She didn't want to be seen. Not yet.

Her aunt stood, stepping on to a small stage that had been put up beneath the staircase and turning to face the audience. "Dear guests," she said loudly. "Dear, dear seekers after truth. Welcome to Carrion Castle and a night of psychic wonders. Prepare yourselves to be amazed – please don't do that there, madam, the toilet is clearly signposted. Where was I? Oh, yes, please, without further ado, welcome my niece ... the

supremely gifted ... the one, the only ... *Mallory Vayle!*"

Shadow play, Mallory thought to herself while she listened to a smattering of polite clapping. It was so easy. She'd start by teasing her audience. Make them wait a little longer.

Slowly to begin with.

She twitched her fingers. On one wall a shadow turned the wrong way, making a woman snap her head around in a double-take. A man blinked as his shadow picked its nose. Around the hall, one, then two, then three more people frowned as they caught strange movements from the corners of their eyes. Heads began to turn.

Mallory smiled to herself. Feeling Hellysh Spatzl's anger growing behind her, she whispered, "Patience. You'll get your ritual. At midnight."

Mallory twitched her fingers again. Around the hall, darkness stretched. The audience gasped as their shadows became tall, slender strangers. Long arms reached out with grasping fingers.

Nervous gasps became frightened whimpers.

Now, let's get this party started.

A shadow burst, fluttering crazily. Then another and another until the grand hall's walls swarmed with

thousands of dark, silent bats.

Applause turned into shocked gasps as shadow peeled away from the walls and began swooping through the air, impossible shadow-bats brushing past faces on wings of nothing.

Good, Mallory told herself, listening to a fresh wave of

applause – more enthusiastic now. Five shillings was five shillings. She owed her audience a few gasps.

At another twitch of her fingers, shadow-fire leapt up, skeletons dancing in the flames. Mallory whispered and – together – the spirits obeyed. "Wooooo," they groaned. "*Woooo.*"

Classic ghost, Mallory thought to herself. Necromancy leaked from her fingertips, sending faint ribbons of purplish darkness through the air. Among the cobwebs, wispy figures became visible, flitting through the rafters like bed sheets with holes cut out for eyes.

Mallory's grin widened as the squealing grew louder below.

With another twitch of her fingers, an enormous, grinning shadow-skull appeared in thin air, glaring down at the crowd. Ghosts flitted through its eye sockets and around its giant wig.

Mallory nodded to herself as squeals became screams. *Enough.*

Mallory waved a hand. Ghosts vanished. Their voices faded out. Shadows returned to normal.

All the shadows except one.

Mallory stepped to the head of the stairs, her own shadow growing until it stretched out from her feet, filling the wall and the high ceiling. A human skull cupped in its hands, Mallory's shadow rippled and swirled; dark hair moving and curling around her shadow-face in a non-existent breeze.

Outside, thunder roared.

Lightning spat.

Perfect timing.

"Good evening," said Mallory, at last.

Evening ... good ... good ... welcome ... to ... Carrion Castle ... good evening ... extravaganza...

In strange echoes, her Voice chased itself around the hall. Every head in the grand hall swivelled to look up at the small figure standing alone at the top of the staircase, holding a skull in one hand, a book tucked under her arm.

Screams trailed off. Silence crowded into the room.

"*Yaas*, Mallory," shrieked an excited voice only she could hear.

She looked down and spotted Maggoty on a chair in the front row. "That is how you make an entrance," he screeched. "Maggoty is *literally* speechless. Completely lost for words. Applause, applause, applause. The big shadow Maggoty was the perfect touch. *Gorgeous.* Let's have a lot more of that. Did Maggoty mention – completely lost for words?"

One hand on the carved banister, chin high, Mallory walked down the grand staircase like a queen of shadows, black eyes sparkling in the light of a hundred candles. "Welcome," she said as she descended, one slow step

at a time. There was no need for her Voice now, and no need to shout. The hall hung with deathly quiet. Even the thunder seemed to be waiting for her next words. Mallory beamed at her audience. "And a very g-g-g-ghoulish night to you all," she continued. "This night, we at Carrion Castle present a carnival of spookiness. Tonight, we open our arms to those who have passed over. Tonight, we will witness marvels and miracles. Tonight, the dead walk again." She paused, turning her smile up a notch. "Not bad for five shillings, eh? Oh, and please don't forget tea and cakes are on sale at very reasonable prices."

Her last words broke the tension. Laughter rippled through the crowd.

Mallory grinned back at her audience, knowing she had them, and hearing Maggoty's voice: "Work it, Boo."

"But first," Mallory went on, taking her time. "Let's have a round of applause for the person who made all this possible. Ladies and gentlemen, Mistress of the Night: *Lilith Nightshade*. Where are you, Aunt Lilith?"

Aunt Lilith stood and turned to the audience with a small bow as they clapped again. Tonight, she had dressed in a floor-length black gown that was tight to the knees before flaring into ruffles at the bottom. Cheap

glass jewels – looking like they were worth fortunes – flickered at her throat and on her wrists. A white streak in her piled-up hair gleamed in candlelight.

Blowing her a kiss, Mallory stepped on to the stage. Setting the skull and book down on the table her aunt had placed there, Mallory twirled to face her audience.

For a few moments she gazed from face to expectant face. They looked eagerly back at her.

Suddenly, Mallory slumped, allowing her head to dangle forward, hair falling over her face. Under her breath, she whispered in a Voice that echoed into the dead dimension: "All right, then, who has messages for this lot?"

Messages ... what news ... speak, spirits...

She groaned – a groan that came straight from her bowels. Lifting her head, Mallory fixed the audience with necromancer's eyes. Dramatically, she put a hand to her forehead. "The spirits are speaking to me," she moaned. "I'm ... I'm getting the name Charlie. Charlie Feet. Is there a Charlie Feet in the room?"

"Here. Here," shouted a sprightly looking old man, springing to his feet and waving an arm. "I'm Charlie Feet."

"I have a message from your wife, Charlie. Esther. Her name was Esther, wasn't it?"

Charlie gasped. "Esther. Yes. She … she passed away three years ago."

"But she's still watching over you, Charlie," said Mallory. "And she has a message. She wants to say…"

Mallory stopped.

Give 'em a show.

"What? What does Esther want to tell me?" squeaked Charlie.

A fresh smile curled Mallory's lips. "Well," she said slowly, raising a hand and allowing a little necromancy to leak from her fingertips. "Why don't we let Esther tell you herself?"

The air in front of the old man gathered into white mist. Mallory heard yet more gasps and chair legs scraping across the floor as people shifted away. Reminding herself there was no hurry, she fed necromancy to the spirit of Esther Feet in a drip. The mist flowed together, slowly becoming a human figure, then a female figure in a floating, wispy nightgown, its hair in curlers, its face glowing with light and good humour.

"Esther!" her husband cried. "My own dear Esther!

I ... I... Oh, *Esther.*"

"What's your message, Esther?" Mallory prompted.

The ghost crossed her arms, fixing her husband with a twinkling glare. "I see you doing that, Charlie Feet," Esther snapped. "Every afternoon at four-thirty. Stop it. Stop it at once!"

CHAPTER 27

Mallory gave them a show. She even sprinkled glitter on it. Beneath golden candlelight she gave them a spooky carnival of laughter and tears, thrills and spills. She channelled spirits. Ghosts walked the hall of Carrion Castle, greeting friends and family they had left behind. Old arguments were put to rest and ancient jokes cracked once more. Forgotten voices spoke. People looked into the eyes of the dead, weeping goodbyes that had gone unsaid in life.

Mrs Emma Simpleton discovered that she was the last living relative of Dilbert Tinkler, and heir to the Tinkler's Tinned Meat fortune, worth over thirty thousand pounds. Dilbert's ghost was so pleased to meet his

great-grand-daughter he promised the entire audience fifty per cent off Turkey Tinklers.

An off-duty police officer at the back of the hall was visited by the disappointed ghost of Margie Dribble, who gave him the name and address of her son, Rupert, also known as Snaggles, the Stabbings Mugger.

The ghost of Hugh Jankles, an antiques expert wearing half-moon spectacles and a three-cornered hat discovered that Nancy Kipper in the third row was using a rare fourteenth century wasp clamp worth three hundred pounds to dig wax out of her ear.

The audience goggled and giggled in amazement while Mallory fulfilled her promise – spinning spectacles and miracles. It was a night of necromancy, but in Mallory's hands dark, deathly magic was spun into wonder and light. Merriment echoed in the ceiling. Five hundred pairs of eyes glimmered with delight as they looked upon loved ones thought to be long gone. While a storm raged outside, ghosts filled Carrion Castle with warmth, and a few spine-tingling surprises.

At the centre of it all, Mallory sat on a high stool, ignoring the ever-increasing fury of a figure hidden in shadow and flicking necromancy across the room with

deft fingers; inviting ghost after ghost to join the fun while her aunt served tea and cake.

Hours passed.

All the while, the presence of Hellysh Spatzl grew angrier. Sensed only by Mallory, a growing spite settled on Carrion Castle, becoming heavier and heavier until she could no longer ignore it. Hellysh Spatzl had been waiting for this night for five centuries and her shadow was restless. She demanded to be reborn with an insistence that promised death would follow if she went unheeded any longer.

Across the city, bells rang out the midnight hour.

Mallory couldn't put off the ritual any longer. Hellysh's patience had run out.

Ready or not, the ancient shadow of a twisted necromancer was coming.

It was the moment Mallory had been dreading. Her mouth set in a hard line. She bit her lip, tasting blood. Unexpectedly, she caught a memory: the ghosts of her mother and father standing either side of her, making fun of their own funeral.

She missed them so much she could barely draw her next breath.

It was time.

She was ready.

Thunder broke the sky. Lightning turned it into a sheet of white fire.

Mallory climbed down from her stool, lifting her hand. Around the hall, ghosts faded and vanished.

The audience sighed in disappointment. Standing at the front of the stage, her head bowed, Mallory waited until the sound died in a fresh rumble of thunder. More lightning flickered outside the windows. Rattling the frames, drafts billowed cobwebs and fluttered candle flames. "And now," she said. "Now we come to the finale of our Grand Séance." Reaching down, she caught up Hellysh Spatzl's skull and tossed it up, catching it lightly. "Dear guests, I'm sorry. *Deeply* sorry, but I'm afraid you were invited here for more than an evening of spooky entertainment."

Mallory looked from face to face. Smiles faded, laughter died.

"Oh, the *drama*," shrieked Maggoty from the front row. "Oh, oh, oh. Maggoty is going to widdle himself."

"A shadow walks among us," Mallory continued. "A shadow that doesn't care if you live or die." She turned

Hellysh's skull this way and that. "This old bone is all that is left of her body, but this shadow demands I steal your spirits so it can be made flesh again."

Her audience couldn't begin to understand what Mallory was talking about, but they could sense that fun had come to a sudden, juddering end. They could sense too the growing presence of Hellysh Spatzl. Staring from face to frightened face, Mallory felt the colour drain from her own. In the front row, Aunt Lilith was standing, shaking her head: *don't do this.*

Mallory gave her what she hoped might be a reassuring smile. It fell apart on her lips.

"Trust me," she whispered, her voice cracking.

Once again, lightning split the sky in two. Thunder shook the walls of the castle.

Mallory moved her fingers, making the skull in her hand spin slowly. "Why would I do such an awful thing, you might ask?" she said, looking around the sea of scared faces. "Why would I commit such a horrible crime to help this shadow?" She paused, then continued. "The answer is that I'd do it to save my mother and father. Or at least the *ghosts* of my mother and father. This shadow that has murdered again and again, you see. It murdered

my parents and the coach driver bringing them home to me. It murdered Harry Gizzard, who some of you might have known. And – dear guests – those murders are not the last of the shadow's crimes. Now, it – *she* – is holding the ghosts of my ma and da hostage, threatening never-ending torture if I do not create a new body for her so she may weave *more* of her foul magic. She demands I bring her back from the grave. Ladies, gentlemen, dear guests, *that* is why you are here."

Thunder boomed again. In the hall of Carrion Castle nothing moved. No one dared to breathe. Not even Maggoty spoke.

"Hellysh Spatzl," Mallory yelled over the sound of roaring skies. "You have killed. You have blackmailed and cheated and plotted and lied to swindle your way back into the world of the living. Tonight – *NOW* – it is time for your reward."

An unearthly wind blew through the great hall, carrying the flavours of ancient rot and maggoty tombs and the crazy, cackling laughter of Hellysh Spatzl.

As one, the audience gasped in horror. None of them needed to be psychic to smell and hear the evil that approached. Hellysh had saved her strength for this

moment. She was coming.

Thunder rolled again. Howling sheets of rain beat against the window as if the sky itself was angry with the shadow that stalked Carrion Castle. Lightning flashed, flickering on a shadowy figure by the door, hunched and hooded.

With her free hand, Mallory lifted the ancient, leather-bound book. It fell open at a page headed *How to Rayse the Ded*.

For a second, she looked up, straight into terrified violet eyes.

Aunt Lilith had picked up Maggoty Skull and was clutching him to her chest. "Mallory, no," she mouthed silently.

"Aaaarghh, get 'er off me," Maggoty screeched, not quite so silently. "Mallory! Mallsy. Get her off've me. Hey, watch the wig. Maggoty said, *watch the flippin' wig*. Mallory, HELP! Maggoty's in the clutches of a desperate wig knocker-offer!"

Mallory snorted, before looking down at the book again.

Terrified whimpers spread through the audience as Hellysh Spatzl's hideous shadow dragged itself, lurching between rows of chairs towards the small stage where Mallory sat. With every step she gathered what remained of her power, growing more solid, more terrifying, until even the audience could see the hooded figure, trailing shadowy rags and twisting its shadow fingers together in triumph.

After five hundred years in shadow, Hellysh Spatzl's moment had finally come.

Again, Mallory glanced down at the book in her lap, then at the skull in her hand, then at Hellysh's shadow. Everything she needed to complete the ritual was in place. She could feel necromancy throbbing through her veins. With a few words, she could release a tidal wave of dark magic and raise Hellysh back to life.

"Stop," said Mallory, her voice quiet but her Voice ear-splitting.

STOP ... STAY ... I COMMAND ... STOP ... STOP ... STOP.

A few feet from Mallory, the horrible figure of Hellysh Spatzl stopped. Gnarled shadow hands curled into claws.

Mallory allowed the echoes of her Voice to die away before speaking again. "I promised I would join your shadow to your bones, didn't I?" said Mallory matter-of-factly. She tossed the skull in one hand.

Hellysh's shadow made a screeching noise of pure hatred. *"Yessssss,"* she hissed. *"Now."*

Mallory sat back down on the stool, taking time to make herself comfortable before speaking again. "I have these two things," she said quietly. She lifted the book in one hand: "Book." In the other she raised

the skull: "Bones."

Mallory paused, then went on. "*Your* book, Hellysh. *Your* bones. You gave me everything I need to bring you back from the dead," she said, smiling. "But that's not *all* you gave me, is it?"

"Your parentsss," Hellysh growled. "Do it ... do it nowww ... or they will *ssssuffer.*"

Mallory ignored her. "No," Mallory went on. "That's not all you gave me. You gave me *options* too. Did it ever cross your twisted mind what else I could do with *this* book and *these* bones?" Resting the skull on the small table next to her, Mallory licked her thumb and turned back a page slowly, while Hellysh's shadow looked on, caught in a web of Mallory's Voice and her own horrified fascination.

"*Whaat?*" she hissed.

Again Mallory ignored her. She turned another page. Then another. And another. Finally, she stopped. For a moment her smile widened. She looked up, eyes bright with necromancy. "What's this?" she chuckled. "The spirit prison, hmm? A most amusing curse of your own invention."

"STOP THIS *MADNESS*—" Hellysh began. The long,

drawn-out hiss had vanished from her voice.

Mallory shrugged, unconcerned. Looking down at the page again, she interrupted, "It says here that all I need is bones. It says that a skull makes an attractive decorative object." Mallory reached out and picked up Hellysh's skull again. "A skull like this, maybe?"

"You would not—"

Mallory scowled, interrupting again. "No, you're right. I would never, *never* willingly use this vile curse – not even on *you* – so I'll give you a choice. Release my parents. *Go*. Finally accept death as you should have done five hundred years ago, and never return. Or suffer the same punishment you gave Matthew."

"Your parents. Your mother ... your father."

Mallory tilted her head. "Really? You're going *there* again. You've lost, Hellysh. Release my parents then die. Fade away. *Leave*, you wretched hag. It's the best offer you'll get tonight. Because once you're trapped in your own skull you'll be powerless, hmm? Not even magic can escape. You won't be able to hold my parents from me any longer."

Hellysh hesitated. It was all Mallory needed to know that she was right. "Release them and go, Hellysh," she

whispered, lifting the skull a little. "It's that or spend for ever in here, just like Matthew."

"Curses on you. Curses on your offer. I will make you suffer. Everyone will *suffer*—"

Mallory leaned forward. In a whisper, she interrupted, "Very well. If you won't release my mother and father then I'll take them from you. Remember, I gave you a choice."

Hellysh's shadow was whirling now, looking for escape.

"Stay," said Mallory.

Stay ... do not move ... there ... stay there...

"A suitable punishment, eh?" she continued, her voice dropping to a murmur only the shadow could hear. "I didn't want to do this, Hellysh. I'm not like you. But just between us necromancers there's a part of me that's going to enjoy it. To tell you a secret: it's quite a *big* part."

At the last moment, what remained of Hellysh Spatzl tried to flee, but Mallory's Voice had become too powerful – more powerful than any shadow stretched thin over five centuries could hope to resist. Still Hellysh struggled, screaming.

Calmly, Mallory looked down and began to read: "Bone and tyme in a pryson combyne..."

It was deep necromancy. Watched by five hundred open-mouthed people, Mallory spun magic in blood reds, midnight blues and deepest purples around the room; words echoing and repeating over and over while she added new ones from the book in front of her. Holding down the fluttering pages in her lap, she weaved whirling, deathly magicks. Necromancy bubbled from her stomach and spilled over her lips in floods.

Ribbons of dark magic spun, flashing colour.

Mallory closed her eyes. Necromancy poured from her in unstoppable gushing waves. All of it focused on the shadow at the centre of a magical whirlwind.

Gasping at the hideous taste of the words in her mouth, she almost stopped.

Hellysh had killed her parents, Mallory reminded herself and forced the final – awful – words through her teeth.

A dark quiet fell.

The universe held its breath.

Forks of lightning smashed through the high windows, showering the crowd below with broken glass.

Sound crashed back into the world in a tornado of screams and thunder.

Jagged, crackling spears of lightning hit the shadow of Hellysh Spatzl at exactly the same moment. At the centre of a blaze of impossible black light, the shadow stopped struggling and gazed in horror at a glowing padlock that shimmered into existence before her face.

Mallory threw the skull in her hand into it.

Hellysh's mouth opened in a silent scream.

Shadow collapsed in on itself, and was sucked into a dark keyhole. The padlock snapped shut.

All necromancy vanished, leaving just a skull spinning on the checked tiles of Carrion Castle with a *roin-roin* sound. Deep within its eye sockets, tiny points of light flared, as red as hot metal, burning with fury.

"Anita Pea," Mallory breathed before exhaustion swept over her. She tried to rise from her stool and stumbled back.

Silence.

More silence.

Around the great hall people sat up straighter.

The babble of voices shook the cobwebs above: "Did you see—", "The stage trickery was fabulous—", "Actually thought Mother was in the room—", "When the windows broke a little bit of wee came out—", "People on the roof with some kind of electrical thingummybobs, I suppose—", "Best spectacle I've ever seen—", "The part at the end was taking it a bit far, I thought—"

Around the hall, people started doing what people do: they explained away supernatural shenanigans, putting ghosts and spooks and things that go bump in the night back where they belonged: in stories. They stopped being frightened children and started being people again.

And Aunt Lilith understood people.

Setting down Maggoty's skull, and absent-mindedly brushing wig gack from the front of her dress, she climbed on to the stage. Raising her hand for silence, she smiled and held out a hand towards her niece. "Ladies and gentlemen," Aunt Lilith called, "I give you the psychic stylings of the astonishing, the incredible *Mallory Vayle*. You've been a wonderful audience. *Goodnight*, and please come back soon for another amazing Grand Séance."

People began to clap. The claps turned into a cheer. Dazed, deafened by applause, stumbling, and with tears pouring from her eyes, Mallory allowed her aunt to pull her to the front of the stage where they both took a bow.

Behind them, the wide-eyed ghost of Sally Vayle looked out over the sea of cheering people and whispered to her husband, "What on *Earth* has Hilda got our Mallory into?"

CHAPTER 28

Weeks passed. After the tearful reunion and all stories and explanations had been told, Mallory began to notice the little things. It was the way her mother rolled her eyes while trying to start a conversation with another ghost; the way the smile fell off her face when she thought Mallory wasn't looking.

There was a sadness about her parents now she had never seen before. They tried to hide it but she had caught her father staring out of windows. Once, she had heard him whisper, "*Woo,*" as if trying out the sound of it.

It had almost broken her heart.

Added together, it all meant one thing: family meeting. The Grand Séance had made a *lot* of money. Aunt

Lilith had put the cash to work. Teams of cleaners and decorators had whirled dusters and paint brushes. Carrion Castle was changing. A little. Most of the rickety old castle was still a ghost story waiting to happen, but in the grand hall the chandelier burned brightly every night now. Polish gleamed on the checkered floor tiles and fresh paint covered the walls where portraits of long-dead people who had nothing whatsoever to do with Carrion Castle hung. Her aunt had simply bought whatever old paintings she could find in the bric-a-brac shops of Stabbings. A fire burned in a vast fireplace. Maggoty had helped pick out acceptably stylish furniture.

"I like your headscarf, Aunt Lilith," said Mallory, as her aunt settled herself on the edge of a new sofa. "Dangly earrings too. *Classic* psychic."

"She looks a right pranny," muttered Maggoty from his new wooden stand near the fire. Mallory hadn't told him but it was a bird table she'd found in a second-hand shop. She'd scraped off the droppings and told him she'd had it specially made.

"Maggoty says you look fabulous," added Mallory.

"Thank you, darling." Her aunt shot the skull a

suspicious look. Her eye twitched. Returning her attention to Mallory, she said, "What's this all about, hmm? It's all *sooo* mysterious."

Aunt Lilith shivered suddenly and touched her neck.

The ghost of her mother appeared and settled on to the sofa not far from her sister. "Yes, what's so important, Mallory?" she asked, forced jollity in her voice. "Busy, busy, busy. Haunting to do."

"It's about *you*, actually," said Mallory. Glancing at her father who was practising touching the back of her aunt's neck with ghostly fingers, she added, "Stop that, Da. Pay attention, please."

While her father sighed and floated round to perch on the arm of the sofa next to his wife, Mallory did something she had avoided in the weeks since the Grand Séance. With a twitch of fingers, she leaked necromancy into the room. Her eyes grew a little darker. Aunt Lilith made a small *meep* sound, clutching her chest as Mallory's parents became visible. Green lights flared brighter in Maggoty's eye sockets. Because he was family too.

"Family meeting," Mallory announced, walking to stand with her back to the fire, next to Maggoty.

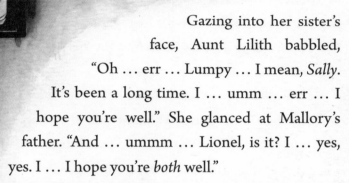

Gazing into her sister's face, Aunt Lilith babbled, "Oh ... err ... Lumpy ... I mean, *Sally*. It's been a long time. I ... umm ... err ... I hope you're well." She glanced at Mallory's father. "And ... ummm ... Lionel, is it? I ... yes, yes. I ... I hope you're *both* well."

"We're dead," said Sally Vayle. "Apart from that we're both in excellent health, thank you, Hilda."

"It's Lili..." Aunt Lilith stuttered to a stop. "Actually, never mind. *Hilda*. Of course."

The ghost of Sally Vayle smiled. "And 'Lumpy' is just fine, Hilda," she said, patting her sister's knee with wispy fingers.

"Ugh, *gross*," muttered the skull. "If everyone's being – bleurgh – *nice* to each other, you'll have to excuse Maggoty while he pukes. *A-wop-bop-a-looma*."

Her father grinned. "I *love* that skull," he chuckled.

"Family meeting," Mallory repeated in a firm voice that only wobbled slightly. "Please pay attention."

Her aunt and ghostly parents looked at her, expectation in their faces. "It's ... well." Mallory stopped, tears beginning already pricking at her eyes. "Ma. Da. I ... I..." She stumbled again, unable to find the right words, then blurted: "You shouldn't be ghosts."

Her mother squealed. "*Mallory!* You're not to bring us back from the grave. What would the neighbours say? 'Oh, look, it's the Vayles. Didn't we bury them a few weeks ago?' It would be awkward. Embarrassing."

Lionel Vayle nodded. "Your mother is right," he said. "Though if you could bring me back for, say, one afternoon, I'd love to see old Whuppley's face when I shambled into the bank, arms outstretched, groaning, *'Braaaaaains.'* Or, *'Buuuums.'* Yes, *'Buuuums,'* would be better. Wrap a few bandages round me and I could groan at him that I'd been *bummified*. An abumination from beyond the grave. That would be a laugh." Pausing, he added, "Because – you know – bum problem."

"Yes, Lionel," Sally Vayle sighed. "We got it. Now shush, dear. Mallory, you're to do no such thing."

Mallory shook her head. Voice shaking too, she said

quietly, "It's all right, I don't want to bring you back. That's not what I was going to say."

"Well, what then?" Her mother looked confused. "There aren't any other options for us, are there?"

Mallory paused again, biting her bottom lip. The words she needed to say did not want to be said.

Luckily, her aunt was there to help.

"*One*," said Aunt Lilith, giving Mallory a look of understanding. "There's one other option. Isn't there, darling?"

Nodding gratefully, Mallory murmured, "Yes."

While her mother and father blinked at her, Mallory forced herself to go on, faltering over the words she had prepared so carefully. "I ... I don't want you to be ... well, *ghosts*. I don't want to be Daisy Hadley, keeping you stuck here when you should be somewhere else. You should ... move on. How do you say it, Aunt Lilith?"

"Go into the light, dear."

"That's it. Go into the light." Ignoring the stunned looks on her parents' see-through faces, she stammered on. "It's ... it's ... just that even though you're dead, you both have too much life in you to be wafting around haunting a world that can't see you any more."

"We can't just *leave* you, Mall," said her da, shaking his head.

"Yes. Yes, you can," Mallory insisted. "I ... I will be ... well, maybe not fine but I have Aunt Lilith now. And M-Maggoty. He'll look after me. Won't you, Maggoty?"

The skull managed to look thoughtful. *"Weeeell,"* he said after a couple of moments. "Depends what you mean by 'look after'. If you mean 'giggle in a corner while you get yourself mixed up in all sorts of dangerous paranormal shenanigans', then, yup, Maggoty's defs the skull you're looking for."

"He'll look after me," said Mallory, as firmly as she could while blinking back tears. "And Aunt Lilith too."

"Of course, dearest," said her aunt.

Sally Vayle stood and floated over to her daughter, wrapping insubstantial arms around her. "No, Mallory. We promised, remember? And your father's right. We just can't."

"Yes, you can," Mallory repeated, looking up into her mother's eyes. "And you *should*. It's not that I don't want you to stay. I'll miss you. I'll miss you *so* much. Both of you. But you ... you belong elsewhere now. I don't know where exactly, but I know it's not here. I think you know it too."

"I can't imagine what you're talking about," said her mother, though she couldn't look Mallory in the eyes.

"I think you can," Mallory insisted, before turning to her father. "You know, don't you, Da?"

Looking a little guilty, her father said, "It's like a tugging feeling, isn't it, Sally?"

Her mother made a face. Nodding, she whispered, "Yes. Like there's an adventure waiting and we're about to miss the train."

"Don't miss it," Mallory whispered, tears brimming over her eyelashes and rolling down her cheeks. "I don't want you to miss it."

Her father wafted over and took his wife's hand. "Mallory's right, isn't she?" he said, his voice gentle. "This isn't our place now."

Heartbreak plain on her face, Sally Vayle whispered, "You're sure, Mallory?"

"I'm sure," Mallory said before she could stop herself and beg them to stay. "It's ... it's what is *supposed* to happen. I'm supposed to miss you and you're supposed to find whatever is waiting."

Aunt Lilith cleared her throat. "At least we *know* something is waiting," she said. "Not many people get that wonderful crumb of comfort, and you don't need to worry about Mallory. I shall be a guardian angel watching over her."

"Thank you, Hilda," choked Sally Vayle. "And if ... if we're saying goodbyes, I should say I ... I'm sorry I wasn't a very good sister."

"And neither was I," said Aunt Lilith, blinking back tears of her own. "When the time comes I hope we can make that up to each other."

"I'll look forward to it," said Sally Vayle. Looking back at Mallory, she said simply, "When?"

"*Now*, I think," whispered Mallory. "If you stay any longer, I don't know if I'll be able to say goodbye."

"I don't know how to say goodbye now," her father croaked, floating closer.

"Me neither," sobbed her mother.

"Like this, perhaps," murmured Mallory, tears in her voice. Digging deeper than she ever had before into the well of necromancy that burned in her stomach, she opened floodgates of dark power and poured it into her parents. Wave upon wave of magicks swirled around them, bringing them closer and closer to the world of the living, for just a few moments.

Aunt Lilith gasped as her sister and the brother-in-law she never knew she had grew less wispy around the edges. Colour spread across their faces and into their clothes. They became – for a few seconds – almost solid.

And at last, Mallory felt her parents' arms around her again.

"Goodbye," she whispered, gasping with effort. It was too much. Feeling her knees begin to buckle, Mallory let go.

Her necromancy was spent. The ghosts of her mother and father began to fade. Lights dimmed in Maggoty's eye sockets.

Voices catching in their throats, her parents whispered their last ghostly farewells.

As their spirits left the world behind, Mallory heard her father say, "On the other side, do you think ... do you think I'll be able to learn the bongos, Sally? I always wanted to play bongos."

"You are not going to learn the bongos, Lionel," said the fading voice of Sally Vayle. "You'll upset the neighbou—"

And then they were gone.

For a moment there was silence. Maggoty Skull broke it, saying, "You never told Maggoty your da was such a goober, Mallsy-Bum. Runs in the family, does it?"

Mallory cuffed him gently, knocking his wig over one eye socket. "Shut up, Maggoty," she said, wiping her eyes with a free hand.

Aunt Lilith dabbed at her own tears with a black, lacy handkerchief. "That was very brave of you, sweetheart," she said. "And it must have been ever so difficult. Let Aunt Lilith take you out for dinner, hmm? It won't make any real difference, of course, but better to be sad with a full tummy than sad and hungry, don't you think?" She gave Maggoty a glance and added hopefully, "Just the two of us."

Mallory nodded. She needed to get back to whatever passed for normal at Carrion Castle as quickly as possible. Not having to eat her aunt's cooking was a bonus. "And Maggoty?" she said, pretending not to have seen her aunt's glance. "Can he come too?"

Aunt Lilith eyed the skull and sighed. "If you promise it won't speak," she said. "And just the wig skull. Not the other one. The wig one is annoying but the other one gives me the absolute willies."

"*Annoying!*" shrieked Maggoty. "The *gumption*! The sheer *nerve* on her! Oh! Oh! It's gonna go *down*. Maggoty insists ... demands ... that you poke her in the eye and waggle your finger around, Mallsy. Go on. If you truly love sweet Maggoty you'll do this one ickle-wickle, teeny-weeny, eyeball-waggling favour for him."

Mallory nodded again, ignoring Maggoty's jabbering. "Oh, yes. I'd almost forgotten about Hellysh. Thank you for reminding me," she said. "I've left her in a box under the stairs for weeks. She needs to be somewhere else too."

"Well, hurry up, darling. And could you let your hair down? Perhaps change into something more... Oh, forget it."

A skull under each arm, Mallory headed into Carrion Castle's maze of passages where cleaners feared to tread. Glowing emerald sparks in Maggoty's eye sockets illuminated Mallory's own footprints in the centuries-old dust ahead.

As usual, he babbled.

"Any chance of shutting up now?" Mallory asked after a while.

"Pff. Poor Maggoty was outrageously attacked by that snot-crusted, wonky-goose-legged sniffer of gerbil breath. Annoying, she called him. *Annoying!* Like *hello?* Look who's talking! Point is, what did Mallory Bumface do about it, eh? Eh? Nothing. *Nothing!*"

"Mmm-hmm," Mallory replied, concentrating on following the trail of footprints.

"All Maggoty asked was for a tiny little eyeball poking,

and just a touch of swirling your finger around in her eye socket. You say you're a friend, but when the chicks are brown and poo comes to shove…"

"Chips are down. Push comes to shove," Mallory interrupted.

"Oh, who cares? No one's interested. The point is, you smell, Smellory."

"And that wig looks awful on you."

"*Oooooooh*, she's bold," Maggoty screeched. "But too far. *Waaaaay* too far. You've crossed a line… Hey. Hang on. Stop twittering on and on, Boo. Isn't this the way to Hellysh's tower?"

"It is." Mallory stopped in an arched doorway, peering into a courtyard tangled with thorns. Here, her footprints had been washed away by the rain but ahead stood a craggy tower. Making her way across the courtyard, she pushed aside a curtain of ivy and climbed some stone stairs.

Green light splashed around Hellysh Spatzl's ancient chamber of bones. At the sound of Mallory's footsteps, bats fluttered. Everything was just as she had left it. The mouldy portrait of a haughty young woman using Death as her puppet leaned drunkenly against the wall.

Furniture and decorations made of bone sent a shiver down Mallory's spine.

Crossing the room, she set Hellysh's skull on the desk and turned it to face her. "I could've left you in a box," she said calmly. "I could've put you in the dungeon and sealed the door up behind me. Instead, I'll show you a kindness you never showed Maggoty. At least here you'll feel at home."

The skull said nothing. Its eye sockets remained dark.

"Maggoty still thinks you should dress her up a bit," said Maggoty from beneath her arm. "One of those clown wigs would look smashing on her. You know the ones: bald but with two big tufts of red hair on either side. That would match her eyes nicely. And some of those spectacles with googly eyes on springs. Maybe a moustache?" Raising his voice, he shouted, "A *moustache*! You'd like that, wouldn't you, Hellysh?"

Hellysh's skull was silent.

Mallory shook her head. "I've already cursed her. I'm not going to make her look like an idiot too."

"Awww, come on, Boo. Just a moustache? Nothing says 'creepy villain' like a twirly moustache."

"No. She'll suffer enough."

"A bag on her head, then. Very stylish."

Ignoring Maggoty, Mallory leaned down and peered into Hellysh's empty eye sockets. "It's not too late, you know," she murmured. "I never wanted to do this. Not even to you. And I'm going to break Maggoty's curse. Somehow, I'll find a way to do it. I could free you too. All you have to do is promise to leave this world and never, ever, return. Everyone dies, and it's long past your turn. You don't need to be trapped in there for ever."

Silence.

With a sigh, Mallory straightened. "Oh, well, I tried," she said over her shoulder, as she hitched Maggoty beneath her arm and headed for the staircase. "Maybe a few years up here alone will change your mind. I'll come and check on you then. In the meantime, enjoy the view."

The door closed.

In the darkness of Hellysh's tower room, eye sockets glowed red. "You'll be back ssssooner than you think," the skull hissed. "*Necromancer!* Did you think you could toss around such power and it wouldn't be noticed? Did you think there would not be *conssssequences*?"

For a moment, the skull cackled. In a whisper, it went on: "Dangers you cannot imagine are coming,

Mallory Vayle. Matthew cannot help. Matthew will betray you before the end. Only Hellysh can help you now. Only Hellysh can show you the path.

"I'll sssseeee you ssssoon, my Mallory," hissed Hellysh Spatzl. "Very sssssooon, my own *precccccious* fleshhh and blood."

Acknowledgements:

As always, monumental thanks to my wife, Emma, who is patient, wise and never-ending fun. Ta, sweetie. Love you.

And to all the great people at Nosy Crow who are massively talented and brilliant at their jobs, and who made me cake. Cake! Hugely appreciated. Plus, m'great agent, Penny Holroyde: always on hand with chat and support. Lastly, a shout-out to Rachel Delahaye, who pestered me to get Mallory and Maggoty into the world. Thank you all.

LOOK OUT FOR

MALLORY

AND

MAGGOTY'S

NEXT

WIG-RAISING

ADVENTURE!

MALLORY VAYLE

MARTIN HOWARD

AND THE CURSE OF MAGGOTY SKULL

nosy crow

ALSO AVAILABLE IN EBOOK AND AUDIOBOOK!